PRAISE FOR *AJAY AND THE MUMBAI SUN*

SHORTLISTED FOR THE WATERSTONES
CHILDREN'S

It is full of colour
smells and sour
JA

This debut and its he
JASBINDER BILAN

I absolutely love it, easily one of my books of the year . . .
ROSS MONTGOMERY

Exhilarating and heart-warming – a story that shows the true power of the pen. Shah's tremendous talent shines on every page.
CARLIE SOROSIAK

Utterly charming, inspiring and gripping. An absolute must-read!
KIERAN LARWOOD

This sensational debut is full of outrage but full of warmth and friendship too.
KEITH GRAY

This high-stakes adventure is full of characters you will love to root for, told with bundles of energy and heart.
THE BOOKSELLER

[An] absorbing debut novel . . .
THE TELEGRAPH

Thrilling . . . It's rather like Emil and the Detectives *transposed from Berlin to Mumbai . . .*
THE TIMES, CHILDREN'S BOOK OF THE WEEK

An addictively lively and heartfelt story for 9+ . . .
THE GUARDIAN

Shah warmly evokes Ajay's love for the written word . . . as compelling as the scandal that Ajay and his friends uncover . . .
THE IRISH TIMES

A MESSAGE FROM CHICKEN HOUSE

We're back with Ajay and his pals – with a lost treasure and dastardly greedy billionaire, the friends once again have to stand up for truth and justice – all with a sense of humour! I love these modern-day Indian tales with their friendships, bravery and all-action plots!

BARRY CUNNINGHAM
Publisher
Chicken House

AJAY AND THE TREASURE OF THAR

VARSHA SHAH

Chicken House

2 Palmer Street, Frome, Somerset BA11 1DS
www.chickenhousebooks.com

First published in Great Britain in 2024
Chicken House
2 Palmer Street
Frome, Somerset BA11 1DS
United Kingdom
www.chickenhousebooks.com

Chicken House/Scholastic Ireland, 89E Lagan Road, Dublin Industrial Estate, Glasnevin, Dublin D11 HP5F, Republic of Ireland

Cover and interior design by Steve Wells
Typeset by Dorchester Typesetting Group Ltd
Printed in Great Britain by Clays, Elcograf S.p.A

1 3 5 7 9 10 8 6 4 2

British Library Cataloguing in Publication data available.

PB ISBN 978-1-915947-04-8
eISBN 978-1-915947-44-4

To Mum, Tomoko San and Sunagawa San,
Sheila and Mike

and

Joanne, Katie, Stacy, Kate, Yoko

and

The Wombats

. . . what is peculiar to our own age
is the abandonment of the idea that
history could be truthfully written.

GEORGE ORWELL

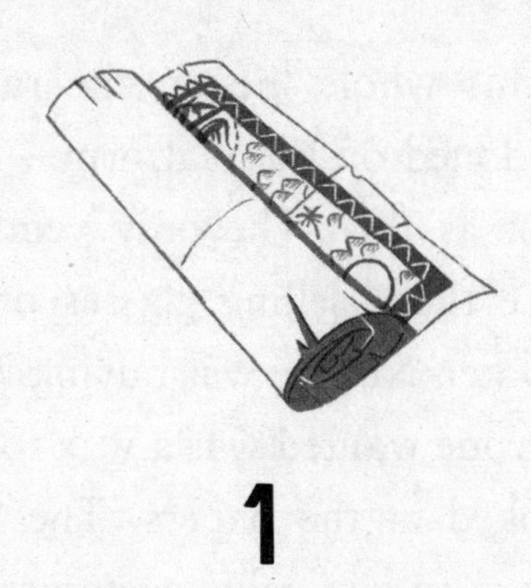

1

The sun radiated down on to the platform at Mumbai railway station. The tracks glowed hot silver, looking as if they were about to buckle and melt, and heat-exhausted early morning commuters stumbled towards their trains pressing bottles of ice-water against their foreheads.

Ajay wiped his brow with his handkerchief and leant against the concrete station pillar – only to jump forwards again as he felt it burn like a clothes iron against his skin. How was it early morning and already so hot? He looked down at the faluda-pink copies of *The Mumbai Sun* – the newspaper he and his friends had created! – and bit his lip. At the age of twelve, or thereabouts, he had spent his whole life on the railways after being abandoned on the platform – it had never been as hot as this! The only vendors making money were those selling glasses of sweet-and-sour lime water. No one was buying *The Mumbai Sun*. All anyone wanted was a way to keep cool.

Ajay looked at the papers. The first rule of business was to give the customer what they wanted . . . a grin spread across his face. He picked up one of the papers and started folding.

Ten minutes later, Ajay looked down with satisfaction, wiping the sweat from his brow. A pile of copies of *The Mumbai Sun* were spread all about him – each one a pink concertina fan! He called out, 'Ten rupees. Ten rupees for a special offer! Two in one: a folded fan with the latest news. Keep cool – and read all about it – in the morning edition of *The Mumbai Sun*!'

From his side came a sharp voice.

'Give me that! I am a businessman—'

Success! Joyfully, Ajay turned and held out one of the fans made out of *The Mumbai Sun*.

The bald-headed businessman snatched it from him.

'—and unlike street kids lazing around all day, I need a cool head to make deals that will bring in money.'

Ajay shaded his eyes from the blazing sun with his hand. 'You are welcome, sir! You now hold in your hand a copy of *The Mumbai Sun* and owe me just ten rupees – a bargain for a newspaper that has taken down a crook, reported a moon landing, and has been edited' – here Ajay gave a modest cough – 'by the humble young man standing before you.'

The bald-headed businessman stopped fanning his face with *The Mumbai Sun*, bent down and looked at Ajay with a crafty glint in his eye. 'Owe you? Ah – but how can I be expected to pay for something that is not in pristine condition? This newspaper has been folded. You cannot expect me to pay for that! Not unless . . .' The businessman's eyes became filled with mist as he looked into the distance, 'you have a story about the Auction Mr Jhoot is holding of his Collection of Marvellous Objects. I would give my life to buy his Collection. Imagine how envious people would be when they came to my home and saw my riches!'

Ajay felt his heart sink. No one – apart from other billionaires – could get tickets to Mr Jhoot's Auction. Even the location of it was Top Secret – and yet it was all that anyone could dream or talk about.

Ajay lowered his voice dramatically, and said in a conspiratorial whisper: 'Kind sir, I don't have a ticket to the Auction.' He took a deep breath. 'But I do have a piece of India's greatest treasures in pristine condition and therefore valuable beyond all measure. If Mr Jhoot knew about it, I guarantee even he would be jealous!'

The bald-headed businessman's eyes widened. 'You own a piece of India's greatest treasures?'

Ajay nodded. 'One definitely worthy enough to get into Mr Jhoot's Auction,' he improvised. 'I found it,' he added for good measure.

'Fallen off the back of a truck?' The businessman's eyes gleamed. 'No – don't tell me. Finders keepers and all that!' He bent down, almost dropping *The* (folded) *Mumbai Sun* in his excitement at his plan. 'Look – your sort can't keep precious objects safe. Sell it to me instead – five rupees should be sufficient for you? After all, anything much more than that and I would have to alert the police – and they don't take kindly to railway kids.'

Ajay stared at him for a moment and held out his left hand. 'Ten rupees.'

Glancing around to check no one was looking, and whipping out his wallet, the businessman handed over the money.

Tucking the ten rupees safely into his pocket, Ajay carefully took the precious object out.

The businessman, who had been rubbing his hands with glee, stopped. 'What's this?'

Ajay smiled at him. 'A seed.'

'What—' the businessman spluttered. 'A seed? But where's the gold? The treasure?' At Ajay's blank look – 'Why you little—'

Ajay smiled at the businessman, cutting his, no doubt grateful, thanks mid-flow. 'You are welcome, sir. It is a seed from a jackfruit tree in the Hanging Gardens. Jackfruit trees are among India's greatest treasures! You don't need to thank me! But your train, sir! You'd better hurry if you want to catch it!'

The bald-headed businessman turned bright

like a jackfruit himself. Then, seeing the train pulling out of the station, he threw the seed down in front of Ajay, and ran to get his seat.

As the train left, with the businessman on it, he waved a clenched fist at Ajay.

Ajay waved back at him, picked up the seed – precious beyond all measure – and tucked it carefully away in his pocket, alongside the businessman's ten-rupee note.

Despite the heat, it was going to be a good day! And afterwards, when he had sold all his papers, to celebrate, Ajay would return to the shade of the Hanging Gardens, eat another dripping gold jackfruit, and plant the seed in the sun-cracked earth. There it would grow – a wonderful, fruit-filled, precious, priceless, one-of-a-kind tree.

Ajay picked up three copies of *The Mumbai Sun* in each hand and fanned himself cool, licking his lips, dreaming of a rain of deliciously golden fruit.

2

Ajay made his way back to the station from the Hanging Gardens, wilting like one of the dying and withered plants he had just seen. He was worried. The heat that was grinding everything in Mumbai to a halt had got worse throughout the day. And the next edition of *The Mumbai Sun* – the finest newspaper in Mumbai – was in trouble because of more than just the heat.

He, Ajay – Editor Extraordinaire – had run out of news!

The last five editions of *The Mumbai Sun* had gone from: *The (Hot) Mumbai Sun*; *The (Hotter) Mumbai Sun*; *The (Hottest) Mumbai Sun*; *The (Extra Hottest) Mumbai Sun*; to, now, *The (Extra*

Extra Hottest) Mumbai Sun. Ajay had been very proud of the titles! But even he had to admit that *The Mumbai Sun* was now sounding more like chilli-pepper sauce than a newspaper . . .

And if he did not find another story soon, the once-mighty paper would soon be pink dust.

As he came up to the platform, Ajay overheard a commuter dressed in a sari talking excitedly to another commuter who was dressed in linen trousers and a shot-silk blouse: 'Have you read it?'

'What?'

'The newest and finest newspaper in Mumbai! You really must read it. It will change your view of Mumbai completely. I don't now read anything else. I have a copy with me – it's called *The* . . .'

Ajay cheered up! He puffed out his chest. Perhaps things weren't so bad after all! *The Mumbai Sun* still had readers! It could still bring voice to the voiceless! It could still—

'. . . *Happy Paper*!' said the commuter in the sari, bringing out a bright, shiny yellow newspaper with a flourish.

The *what*?

Ajay's chest deflated like a popped balloon.

The commuter's friend shrugged loftily. 'No. And I don't intend to. I've made the difficult decision not to read newspapers any more. Reading about poor people makes me feel uncomfortable, especially in this heat. It's so much better to ignore all the unhappiness in the world and concentrate on what I can control and what makes *me* happy.'

'But that's just it!' said the commuter, opening up the bright pages of *The Happy Paper*. 'There is nothing uncomfortable in *The Happy Paper*! It just tells you how you can spend your money, how great billionaires like Mr Jhoot are, and how everything is getting better!'

Ajay's eyes widened.

'All this worry about climate change for example,' the commuter continued – sounding very happy indeed, thought Ajay – '*The Happy Paper* says we have to be impartial and look at both sides. If someone argues that Mumbai is getting hotter, there will be someone else who argues it is not. Both points of view are equal.'

Ajay gaped. That made no sense. Surely if one person told the truth and another told a lie, the truth wasn't somewhere in between?

And also, had *The Happy Paper* not heard of thermometers?

Ajay was about to explain the invention to the commuter in a great amount of detail when a train chugged and whistled its way into the station, the doors lurched open and the commuter and the friend hurried to get in – leaving Ajay standing on the platform, lost and confused.

'Ajay!'

Ajay turned and saw his friend Vinod, one of the older railway kids – tall, lanky, gentle and quiet – waving to him to come over to where he was sitting next to a bubbling pot over a canister flame. Beside Vinod was their friend Jai, also about fifteen – the Slum-Kid Cricketer! – leaning against one of the steps.

'Try some Kashmiri tea!' said Vinod as Ajay came over, pouring dusty-pink tea from the pot to a clay mug. 'I've been practising the recipe. It's—'

'Have you heard of *The Happy Paper*?'

Vinod froze, and some of the tea splashed from the pot, missed the mug and fell to the ground. He and Jai exchanged a look over Ajay's head.

Ajay caught the look. 'You have! How could

you not tell me?' he said, outraged.

Vinod was quiet. He continued to pour more tea into the mug. The rich flavour of cardamom went up Ajay's nose, making him sneeze.

'We were going to—' started Vinod.

'But we didn't want to worry you,' said Jai.

'Worry me?' said Ajay, taking the tea from Vinod despite his annoyance. 'We are *The Mumbai Sun*. We can easily beat this new paper.'

'It won't be that easy, Ajay,' said Jai quietly, his gold eyes dark. 'It's not like other papers. No one outside the station is reading *The Mumbai Sun* any more.'

That stopped Ajay in his tracks. How was that possible? The pink Kashmiri tea sloshed around his mug.

'This new paper's motto is "Opinions Are Great",' Jai continued quietly. 'People like it – more than ours, I think.'

A pit opened in Ajay's stomach. He took a gulp of the hot, fragrant pink tea to steady himself, and rallied.

'We need to show them that they're wrong. Another story! That's all we need. The readers will rush back,' he said brightly. 'Jai – any cricket news?'

Jai shook his head, his hair falling into his eyes. 'All matches have been cancelled because of the heat,' he said bitterly, spinning his cricket bat on the ground with the force of a drill. Taking away his ability to play cricket had left Jai jittery and exhausted. It had been his one outlet; the one place he used to feel safe. Ajay bit his lip, raging helplessly at the weather that was doing what the worst politicians had so far failed to do to those they hated for no reason – cruelly prevent Jai from playing a sport he loved.

And without cricket, what news was left? If *The Mumbai Sun* was going to win back readers it needed a story bigger than Godzilla. Bigger than Everest. Bigger than JUPITER! But the only story that was as big as that was the Collection of Marvellous Objects . . . he looked up.

Vinod looked at him, realization dawning, and shook his head. 'Ajay, it's not possible to get a ticket to the Auction. You know that.'

'We don't need a ticket,' said Ajay, starry-eyed. 'There's another way to get the story!'

3

Why had he not thought of it before? Ajay was beside himself with excitement. The whole of Mumbai knew that Mr Jhoot was holding an exclusive, by-invitation-only, secret party at his apartment tonight. It would be Mr Jhoot's last chance to show off items from his exclusive Collection of Marvellous Objects *before* the objects were sold at the Auction. So, if Ajay and his friends got access to the party, they would get to see and write about the objects too!

Ajay's heart beat wildly. The Collection was rumoured to contain glowing blood-red rubies, the size of fists; silk tapestries so fine they shimmered at every breath; statues carved from sparkling blue-and-white veined marble. Only the cream of Mumbai society had ever seen them. If Ajay could get access to the party, he would have the story of the year – and, better yet, he would be able to show the readers of *The Mumbai Sun* some of the most beautiful examples of craftsmanship in the world. *The Happy Paper* had no chance!

'Forget it,' Jai said quietly.

Ajay was wrenched from his thoughts.

'Jai's right,' said Vinod. 'There's no way *The Mumbai Sun* is getting access to the party. We've tried before, remember?'

Ajay was forced to face facts for a moment. Mr Jhoot – despite being the nicest billionaire in Mumbai – had, again and again, turned down Ajay's requests for an interview (even when they had been written carefully out on the finest faluda-pink paper, in swirling letters, using Ajay's mother's black-and-gold fountain pen!).

'Only the richest and most powerful people in the world get to go to Mr Jhoot's parties,' said Jai, just in case Ajay had missed the point.

Ajay frowned. Jai and Vinod were right. But he

had to do something! *The Mumbai Sun* needed this story if it was to survive. How could he get access? It wasn't as if tickets to exclusive parties in Mumbai just dropped into people's laps.

And that was just it, Ajay realized with dampening spirits – it wasn't just a ticket to the Auction that was impossible to get hold of; even a ticket to the party was too much to ask for. To get some stories you had to be part of the inner circle – and being a railway kid meant that you never could be. So what was left? It wasn't as if great stories were just going to walk in, tug on your arm and announce themselves.

Ajay felt a small pull on his arm.

'Excuse me, kind sir. I am looking for the editor of *The Mumbai Sun*. Do you know where I might find him?'

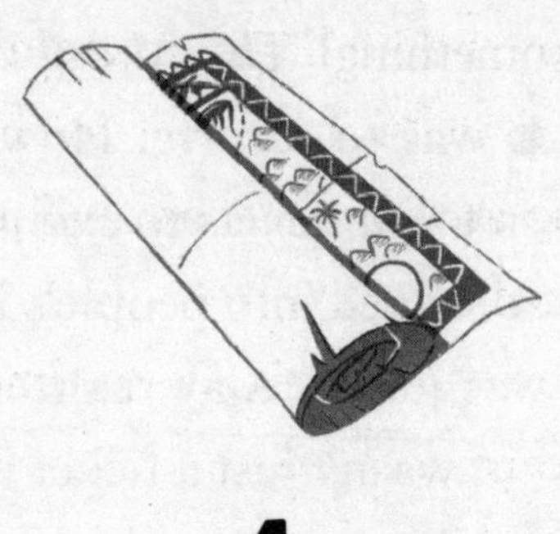

4

Ajay jumped. Then smiled. All was not lost. A fan! Perhaps they wanted his autograph! (He had been practising scrawling it before he went to sleep each night – it had to look good!) He prepared his most serious look and, turning around, spoke slowly and gravely. 'I am Ajay, editor of *The Mumbai Sun*. My pronouns are he/him. I am very pleased to make your acquaintance.'

He held out his hand, blinked, and looked down. In front of him was a young child of about seven years old, wearing shorts, a neatly ironed shirt and glasses, who passed Ajay a note on stiff paper that said: 'Please look after my grandson,

Kai'. The boy would have looked altogether very serious and grave if it weren't for his hair, which was swept up as though a cow had just gone up to him and licked it.

'My name is Kai. I'm my Grandmother's grandson,' he reaffirmed. 'Are you really you?' he asked Ajay. His eyes were wide.

'Of course I'm me!' said Ajay with confidence.

Kai smiled, looking relieved. 'That's good. You see, my Grandmother sent me here to meet you. Now that we've met, you have to come with me.' And, with that, Kai turned and, picking up the heavy suitcase that looked like it was almost his size, started walking.

'Wait!' Ajay cried, quickly taking out his notebook and his mother's pen, and chasing after him. 'Where are we going?'

'To Jodhpur,' said Kai, matter-of-factly.

Ajay stopped in his tracks. 'Jodhpur? But that's in Rajasthan!'

'Yes. It's our first stop, and a very long way away – that's why we have to hurry.' Kai was still walking.

'Stop!' Ajay cried.

Kai stopped and turned around. He looked like he was gathering his strength. Now that Ajay could take a closer look at him, he saw that the frames of Kai's glasses were made of thin wire, one of his shoes had a flapping sole, and that anxiety was rippling under Kai's look of intense determination.

'Will you help me or not?' Kai asked, looking

from Ajay, to Jai and Vinod – who had now caught up – and back to Ajay again. Kai's tone was defiant, but Ajay could see his lip tremble.

'Of course we will!' said Ajay. When somebody needed help, you helped them! And then, suddenly realizing that he needed more information, 'But what with?'

Kai motioned to the three of them to form a close circle around him. Without question, drawn in by his intense look, they did so. The evening sun fell upon him in waves as he took off his glasses, wiped them, and put them on again. Then he coughed, and began to speak in the tones of a British presenter Ajay had seen on the nature documentaries he had become addicted to on the station TV. 'I have travelled for many moons through jungles and mountains—'

'Jungles and mountains?' Vinod said, astonished. 'Where?'

Kai looked at him and frowned. 'Don't interrupt – you'll spoil the story.'

Vinod subsided.

Kai coughed. 'I have travelled for many moons through jungles and mountains to get to you. Me and my Grandmother are the last guardians of the Treasure of Thar.'

Ajay and Vinod looked at each other.

Kai, unperturbed, continued, 'The site of the Treasure was hidden by my great-great-great-grandparents to keep it from being stolen by the British whilst they were busy colonizing India. We have kept the map of its location safe for centuries. Now looters, employed by someone using the seal of a four-headed snake, know of the existence of the Treasure and are trying to find us, and where it is hidden. My Grandmother struggles to move and sent me as a messenger to seek your help. She read a copy of *The Mumbai Sun*. She believes that you are warriors worthy of this sacred quest – to discover the secret of the map that will lead to the exact location of the Treasure, find the ancient Treasure – and then defend it with your lives!' In the golden rays of sunlight, Kai looked very fierce as he said the last words.

'Is this a joke?' Vinod whispered, so that only Ajay could hear.

Ajay didn't answer. He was watching transfixed as Kai, with great ceremony, clicked open his suitcase and took out the only thing in it – an ancient, tattered book with a soft greyish-green cover, held together with string, with gold lettering that spelt *The Traveller's Companion to Thar*. Kai then gently shook the book, so that from the spine slid out a silver metal tube with a screw-top lid. He opened the tube with infinite care, and took out the scrolled piece of paper inside.

A map!

Ajay's eyes widened! He loved maps – maps of the world, maps of India, rail maps, walking maps, tourist maps, road maps, and, best of all, magical maps of fantastic lands that he would sometimes find drawn in the front of books. And this one was beautiful – inked on thick sepia-tinted paper, with a compass rose etched at the bottom and patterns and symbols at the top, and drawings of dragons flying across it. The map showed Jaisalmer Fort on one side and the Thar desert on the other.

And there, marked with a red cross, in the south-west corner of the vast desert, were inscribed the words 'The Treasure of Thar'.

'It can't be real, can it? It has to be a fake,' Vinod exclaimed, earning himself a furious glare from Kai.

Ajay's eyes glowed. A treasure map.

He gently took the map from Kai and stared at it.

It was the miracle he was hoping for!

No, he corrected himself. Not miracle – *miracles*.

A treasure map AND the key to getting in to see Mr Jhoot's Collection of Marvellous Objects.

5

Ajay, Saif, Yasmin and Kai were shooting upwards to Mr Jhoot's apartment in a marble lift. On receipt of Ajay's note (delivered by a butler from the front door), setting out the story of the Guardians and Kai's treasure map, Mr Jhoot had sent back down an invitation to his party!

Saif, apprentice engineer, about twelve and also a railway kid, was busy breathing on one of the lift walls, polishing it with his sleeve to better see his reflection, and beaming at the result. Kai's small face, however, was strained. His reflection showed he was gripping so tightly on to the suit-case, his knuckles were white.

'Are you sure this is a good idea?' said Yasmin, who was standing straight as an arrow next to Ajay. She was also twelve, illustrator for *The Mumbai Sun*, and Ajay's best friend. Her emerald eyes narrowed as she frowned. 'Kai's trusting us to keep his map safe.'

'Of course!' Ajay said. Once he got Mr Jhoot's permission to tell the story of his Collection, *The Happy Paper* would have no chance! Seeing that Yasmin still looked concerned, he added breezily, 'Mr Jhoot is the nicest billionaire in Mumbai! He knows everything about antiques. Who better to tell us if the map is real or not? And if it is real, he'll help us decode its treasure so that it might lead us to the exact location of the Treasure?'

Yasmin looked at him piercingly. 'So, nothing to do with getting a story?'

Ajay was saved from replying by the lift doors opening. For a moment he was stunned into silence.

The party!

He breathed.

What a party!

The doors of the lift had opened into a chilly,

chandeliered, silvery room, with accents of black and turquoise velvet. Jazz music mingled with the sound of clinking glasses, and the room smelt of minerals and ice. People were milling around in silk suits, slithery cocktail dresses splashed with geometrical designs, and saris edged with deep-blue sapphires, the depth and colour of the ocean.

His blood thrumming, and shivering in the suddenly chill air, Ajay took out his notebook and his mother's fountain pen.

'May I put your bag in the cloakroom?' said a cool voice. A tall, elegant attendant had approached Kai.

Kai shrank away, putting his body in front of the suitcase.

'I know something about this,' Saif said confidently. He pushed past Ajay to stand next to Kai, and shook his head at the attendant with an air of hard-earned wisdom. 'No, you may not. Suitcases – even those of apprentice engineers – can get stolen. It is very dangerous to let them out of your sight.'

The attendant arched an eyebrow.

As Saif dealt with the attendant, Ajay looked

around. He needed to find Mr Jhoot.

The crowd was biggest to his right!

'Saif, Yasmin – stay here and find out about the Collection. Kai, you come with me!'

And with that, Ajay and Kai were off, making their way as nonchalantly as they could past tall fluted marble pillars covered in sheets of black velvet. Holding on to Kai's hand, Ajay pushed his way through the crowd (helped by the corners of Kai's suitcase) until, at last, it opened up in front of a person sitting casually on a stool with a smile.

Mr Jhoot!

Ajay – like everyone in Mumbai – had seen countless photos of the billionaire. There was the one of him in a biscuit-coloured safari suit holding a darkly glittering jade mask; the one of him sitting like a mystic on top of a craggy sun-shadowed mountain looking out on to emerald moss-covered ruins; and the one of him underwater in a wet suit and snorkel, swimming beside a towering shipwreck, giving a big thumbs up!

But none of those photos had quite captured the glowing energy that seemed to emanate from him. He sat there, mid-flow, enthralling the audience in his soft voice that sounded like rich coffee dripping into a mug.

'. . . and then I saw it! In the dead of night, by the light of a flickering candle, Tutankhamun's tomb! Full of mystery and wonder – and on it inscribed a curse on those who dared to disturb it . . .'

There were murmurs of *ooh*s and *ahh*s from the crowd.

Ajay could see it now – the warm shadows cast by the gold flame . . . the coppery script . . . a snake slipping out of sight.

'But you couldn't have. There is no curse inscribed on the tomb. It was a made-up story,' Kai's voice piped up, sounding very puzzled.

If Kai had thrown a stink bomb into the middle of the crowd, it would have had less of an effect.

The crowd recoiled as one.

'Who is that?' said Mrs Pritti, a TV presenter Ajay recognized, wearing a lacy blue sari.

'Vermin!' answered someone from the crowd.

'How dare they come here and interrupt? Security!'

Mr Jhoot remained relaxed, a slight twitch of

the mouth the only indication that he had heard. He turned to the crowd and gestured for quiet, his brown eyes warm. 'Please remain calm. They are my guests. And who knows?' He smiled. 'Perhaps this young man is right. After all, isn't that just what I have been talking about? That we must not tie ourselves to one point of view? That we must always be open to debate?'

There was a pause.

Then the crowd rustled like peacocks, their feathers soothed. There was a slow clinking of ice cubes in glasses and a murmuring of relaxed, easy laughter.

Ajay breathed a sigh of relief. He and Kai were safe!

Mr Jhoot truly was the nicest billionaire in Mumbai!

'But I'm right and you're wrong,' cut in Kai.

The laughter stopped.

Ajay gaped. Then he stepped forward hurriedly and coughed, pointing at his name badge. 'I am Ajay, editor of *The Mumbai Sun*. We are sorry to interrupt your discussion, but we have an important matter we need to discuss with Mr Jhoot right away.'

He could hear the sound of blood rushing in his ears. The crowd looked hostile. His words had no effect. In fact, they seemed to have made things worse. He could feel its contempt and instinctively put himself between it and Kai.

At that moment, Mr Jhoot stood and smiled at the crowd, and the threat about to wash over them instantly dissolved. Ajay bristled – irritated rather than relieved. Why did the crowd listen to Mr Jhoot and not to him?

'Another round of drinks, please!' Mr Jhoot said, his smile full of gracious hospitality. In a flash, waiters were pouring golden frothy champagne into the guests' glasses. 'If you will excuse me, I have a small matter to discuss with these two guests and will be back in a moment.'

And before anyone could register what he had said, never mind object, he turned and indicated to Ajay and Kai to follow him, then walked through the back of the crowd that instantly parted for him.

This was it! The chance Ajay had been waiting for!

Ajay took Kai's hand, smiled graciously at the crowd and, with a quick wave and elaborate bow to show that there were no hard feelings, hurried after Mr Jhoot.

6

'This way!' gasped Ajay to Kai, as they pushed their way through the crowd, pointing to Mr Jhoot who was walking to the ice bar in the corner of the room.

An *ICE BAR*? Ajay stopped in shock in front of the huge blue-and-silver slab of thick ice, topped with glasses of silvery drinks and shimmering from the inside with swirling crystal patterns. It smoked frosty blue-and-white air into the room. Ajay stood, open-mouthed, his breath a little puff of white in the chilled air. Here, in Mumbai? In this weather – when people on the streets below were collapsing from heat exhaustion because they couldn't afford to stay cool?

But there was no time to ask questions. As Mr Jhoot walked forwards, two grim security guards parted, and what had seemed to be a wall of expensive crystal bottles swung open. Mr Jhoot entered the secret room.

Staring at each other in awe, Ajay and Kai hurriedly ran and followed him through the door.

It swung shut behind them with a clang.

All the noise from outside was wiped out.

The lights switched on.

'Welcome to my private study,' said Mr Jhoot, smiling.

Ajay could not reply. It was like being in another world. The study was beautiful – and as warm as the room was cold. It was wood-panelled and lit with green lamps, soft rugs in jewel-bright colours cast over the floor.

On one wall was a painting of a bridge, blurred in fog, that seemed to glimmer enchantingly in a wash of blue and green; on a pillar was a sculpture of a golden egg encrusted with shards of diamonds and sapphires pulled by a cherub with feathery wings on a gold-edged chariot; and open on a table, was a manuscript inscribed with swirly ink-blotted writing.

'*Love's Labour's Won*,' said Mr Jhoot, seeing Ajay staring at the book. 'One of Shakespeare's plays. Haven't read it myself, but I expect it is quite good. Look, why don't we sit down and you can tell me all about this map?'

They all sat down on the sofas. Mr Jhoot sat down with elegant grace; Ajay bounced down into the plush comfort, taking out his notebook and mother's pen; Kai sat down gingerly on the edge, his arms wrapped protectively around his suitcase.

For a moment Ajay ached that Yasmin was not with them. He could imagine the high bones of her face soften with tenderness as she took in the beauty all around her.

'Why don't you let slum kids see these treasures?' demanded Ajay. 'It would make us so happy!'

Mr Jhoot leant back, relaxed. 'It's not how the world works, Ajay. The majority of artworks are held in private collections. And those in public collections are often hidden from view. The Royal Collection Trust in Britain, for instance, has a collection of more than one million works, yet only the tiniest fraction of them have a location tag. Without a location tag, the public can't even find out where they may be seen. Now, if British royalty can get away with it, surely so can I?'

Ajay bit his lip, trying to think it through.

'Have a biscuit?' said Mr Jhoot, passing a plate. Ajay put down his pen and notebook and took one. The biscuit was like a work of art itself – a base of slivered almonds in syrup, covered in layers of chocolate and studded with sweet juicy cherries. Ajay munched it appreciatively.

'A beautiful fountain pen,' said Mr Jhoot, eyeing where it lay on the table. 'May I?'

Before Ajay could say anything, Mr Jhoot had picked up Ajay's pen and was turning it over in his hands. 'Truly magnificent. With a remarkable heritage, I think.' Mr Jhoot looked at Ajay and added casually, 'I don't suppose it is for sale?'

Ajay shook his head, his tongue thick at the memory of his mother giving it to him, promising to return for him. She never had. Unable to speak, he stretched out his hand. Mr Jhoot smiled and returned it to him. 'Perhaps another time,' he murmured. 'And now,' he said, turning to Kai. 'I understand that you have a map to the legendary Treasure of Thar. Could I look at it?'

Kai turned to Ajay, his eyes round and large.

'It's OK, Kai,' said Ajay, trying to shake off the numbness. 'Mr Jhoot is just trying to help us. Don't you want to know more about the map?'

Kai swallowed. Unlocking the suitcase, he brought the map out from where it was rolled up into the spine of the book, and carefully handed it to Mr Jhoot.

'Well?' asked Ajay.

Mr Jhoot held it open. For a moment, the only sound was the crackle of parchment paper. In the green glow cast by the lamps, Ajay thought he saw a slight tremor of excitement pass through Mr Jhoot's hands. But the moment passed and, when Mr Jhoot looked up, the expression in his crinkled eyes was that of deep sympathy. 'The map was given to you by your Grandmother?' he asked Kai. 'She lives in Mumbai?'

'Jodhpur,' corrected Kai proudly.

'Ah – I'm sorry. Jodhpur.' Mr Jhoot looked at him and hesitated. Ajay could sense him adjusting what he had been about to say. 'Well, Kai. This map, which suggests the Treasure is in the south-west corner of the desert,' his eyes glowed and then dimmed, 'and which I know you have every reason to think is real—'

'Because it *is* real!' Kai cut in, his cheeks flaming.

'Of course it is.' Mr Jhoot looked to Ajay, and the slight shrug of his shoulders telegraphed his meaning. He did not believe the map was real – but he couldn't say that in front of Kai. Ajay's hopes plummeted. He put his hand on Kai's shoulder.

The door to the study opened, and an assistant, dressed sharply in black, with long hair twisted elegantly in a coil with sharp hairpins, murmured, 'It is time, sir.'

Mr Jhoot nodded, then came to a decision. He stood up smoothly, still holding the map, his face radiating kindness. 'Kai, I tell you what. Why don't you and Ajay stay here and eat more of those biscuits, whilst I take your map—'

Kai's brows slanted downwards.

'Only for a little while, I promise!' Mr Jhoot added quickly. 'In order to get to the bottom of this? After all, who am I to say for sure whether it is real or not? There are some experts outside who will be willing to share their knowledge of cartography. They may see something in the map that you and I cannot. They'll take it seriously if they think it is from my collection rather than belonging to you.'

'Why?' demanded Kai, his frown slanting even deeper.

Mr Jhoot shrugged. 'It is how the world works, I'm afraid. People are trained to listen to the wealthy and powerful. Now, will you give me a chance to help you?'

It was their last shot, thought Ajay. Twice as old as Kai, it was his duty to impart advice gleaned from years of experience and wisdom. He coughed magisterially and, when Kai took no notice of him, elbowed Kai in the ribs. 'I think you should.'

Kai bit his lip and scratched his head.

Then, after a long, long pause, during which Ajay held his breath, Kai gave a small, unhappy nod to Mr Jhoot.

'Excellent!' said Mr Jhoot, turning quickly to the door. 'I just have to give a little speech outside.

I'll ask the experts straight after, and be right back!' And with that he slipped away, disappearing out of the room with the door sliding smoothly shut behind him.

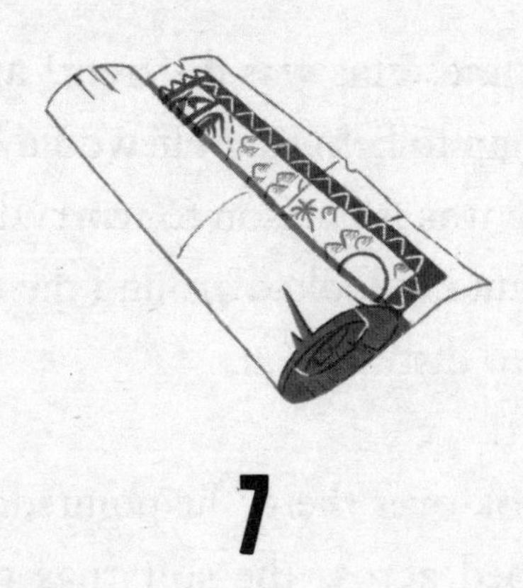

7

For a moment, Ajay wasn't sure what to do. The room, suddenly silent, seemed to change into a shadowy, flickering place.

And Kai, with his arms wrapped around himself, and his eyes screwed tightly shut behind his glasses, seemed very small.

As Ajay looked on, a memory of a recurrent nightmare he'd had – ever since his pen had almost been lost for ever to a mysterious buyer from Switzerland – clenched his insides.

His mother's pen flying out of his grasp. Up and up – higher and higher – twisting, whirling, spinning out of sight until . . .

No! Ajay shook his head, bringing his thoughts

firmly into line. This was different! Mr Jhoot had taken the map to help Kai! He would bring it back soon. There was no reason to worry. Ajay jumped off the couch and looked around the room to find something to distract Kai.

He had it!

'Kai – look over there,' he pointed. 'A globe!'

He stepped across the soft rugs to get to the pearl-white globe that stood next to the desk, and beckoned Kai over. After a deep gulp of air, Kai dragged himself off the sofa and came to stand with him. They both stared. The globe was worth staring at. As tall as Ajay, it glowed with an inner light, its milk-soft radiance dispersing the shadows. Each continent was inlaid with diamonds, and each major city marked with a single sapphire which glistened and sparkled when they caught the light, as if the globe had been made of pulverized stardust. Unable to stop himself, Ajay put his hand on the cool, glassy surface and spun it slowly on its axis and, as the continents shimmered and danced in front of him, for a moment he forgot where he was. He was an adventurer, sailing across the seven seas, spotting bright white polar bears launching off glittering blue ice caps in Canada; burnished gold-tipped condors sweeping across the skies in Peru; emerald-green scaled crocodiles in Kenya; red-faced monkeys in steaming hot springs in Japan; bronze-eyed wolves in Europe; and, best of all, fierce-toothed wombats in Australia.

He would have spun the globe for ever, but for Kai's hand that slammed on to its surface, his face full of anguish. 'Look!'

For a moment, Ajay couldn't understand what Kai was looking at. All he could see was the surface of the globe and his reflection rippling across it. But then he saw the seal of a four-headed snake that Kai had spoken about when they'd first met, etched in silver on part of the globe.

'Ajay!' A high note of panic.

Ajay felt a cold rush of sweat on the back of his neck and shuddered. 'It can't be . . .'

He touched the insignia with horror. It linked the looters trying to steal the Treasure with Mr Jhoot: the sign of a circle and, inside it, the image of a four-headed snake that looked as if it were about to strike.

8

The looters and Mr Jhoot.

Mr Jhoot and the looters.

The four-headed snake insignia could only mean one thing – the looters worked for the so-called nicest billionaire in India.

No wonder Mr Jhoot had been happy to see Ajay and Kai! He was behind the looters; he was behind the threats to find out the location of the Treasure of Thar! And now, because of Ajay, he didn't even need threats – he had Kai's map directing him to the south-west corner of the Thar desert where the Treasure could be found.

Dripping ice-cold with guilt, Ajay turned to Kai.

But Kai had gone – running full-pelt towards the door, hammering it with his tiny fists. He turned to Ajay, his voice caught in between a sob and a shout: 'It's locked.'

Panicked, Ajay took a running jump and threw his weight on to the door . . . wincing in pain as his shoulder smashed against it. He shook his head to clear the blood rushing into his ears.

Keep calm.

This was Mr Jhoot's private study. Mr Jhoot would not risk getting himself locked in. Which meant . . . there had to be a way to release the door from the inside. Ajay looked up, and at Mr Jhoot's eye height, to the right of the door, saw a round panel with the insignia of the four snakes.

He tried to reach it, but couldn't.

'Kai!'

Kai looked at him furiously, his face a mixture of tears and snot, but as Ajay pointed, he understood, launched himself at Ajay and clambered up him.

'Ow!' Ajay cried as Kai's sandalled foot jammed on to his nose, his hands tugged on Ajay's hair, and he stood on Ajay's shoulders.

Balanced on Ajay's shoulders, Kai ignored him. There was the sound of a tile being pushed to one side. His feet did a little hopeful jig that made Ajay yelp. 'It's a keypad. With numbers.'

Kai started pressing all the numbers at once, creating a furore of electronic sounds and lights as he muttered accusingly: 'Grandmother trusted you!'

Ajay felt the words stab him. Shifting, so that Kai's feet were less jabby, Ajay forced himself to think through the hurt. What could the number be?

He had to think like Mr Jhoot.

Four snakes!

'5555!' Ajay shouted up.

Kai hit the numbers. Ajay held his breath.

What if it didn't work?

What if they were stuck for ever?

What if . . .

The door opened.

Ajay released his breath.

Then guilt hit him again like a hammer – the map!

9

Kai jumped off Ajay's shoulders and started to run. Ajay grabbed him by the collar and said pleadingly, 'Mr Jhoot will have bodyguards. We can't get caught before we get the map back.'

'Why should I listen to you?' Kai looked up and shouted at him furiously. 'This is all your fault.'

Ajay felt feverish.

Sick with shame, he bent his head. What could he say to make this better?

Nothing.

Mr Jhoot knew the corner of the Thar desert to look in, but to find its exact location he would have to discover the hidden secrets of Kai's map. They had to get it back before that could happen.

'We need to get your map back and warn your Grandmother about Mr Jhoot. We can't get caught,' Ajay pleaded again, softly.

Kai gave him a look of burning resentment but stopped trying to run.

They stumbled out of the hidden office and were back in the world of the party – the laughter, the clinking of glasses, the different strands of conversation. The jazz band was still playing in the corner. The lead saxophonist, with closed eyes, was playing strands of music that wove together and swept around them in dancing silver and golden notes.

Ajay focused grimly. He could see Mr Jhoot moving towards a raised platform, surrounded by bodyguards. They had to steal back the map before Mr Jhoot disappeared from view. Ajay needed to find Yasmin and Saif, before it was too late. He could imagine it now! His friends jelly with worry about him and Kai; bravely holding back their tears as they wondered anxiously where their best and oldest friend (Ajay!) was; their minds unable to focus on anything other than the task of saving him.

'Ajay!' said Saif's voice cheerfully from behind him.

Ajay turned around, ready to be clasped in Saif's arms in relief. But Saif's arms were full – with a large silver plate piled high (and next to him a trolley that he must have somehow manoeuvred through the crowds) with glittering cakes of pistachio and rose, fondant icing and sugar. He was beaming, and there was a touch of whipped cream on his nose. 'Ajay, this is a wonderful party! Just what an apprentice engineer like myself needs to relax.'

'Saif—'

Saif ignored him, his full attention on the trolley. 'These cakes have been made by a chef who has been flown all the way from France! They had a very silly system in place where waiters took ages coming around with a plate and kept missing me out, even though I kept telling them I was an apprentice engineer.' Saif looked a little affronted at the memory. Then his cheeriness was restored. 'So I solved the problem by finding the trolley in the back and bringing the cakes out to eat instead. It is a solution that only an apprentice—'

'Saif – where's Yasmin?' Ajay cut in urgently.

'Right here,' said Yasmin, coming up to them, her sketchbook in hand. She took one look at Kai's face, put her arm around his shoulders, and glared at Ajay accusingly. 'What's happened?'

Saif looked from Yasmin, to Kai, to Ajay, and silently popped another cream puff into his mouth.

Before Ajay could speak, the room went black. Mr Jhoot's rolling, rich voice boomed out at them in all directions from speakers.

'Distinguished guests. Thank you for being here today. And welcome to my Collection of Marvellous Objects!'

Drum rolls began to play over the speakers and bright spotlights switched on. Ajay blinked and raised his arm to shield his eyes as the beams swept across the crowd, the light rippling over them like a sea of silver water.

The drum rolls stopped; the spotlights fell on to the marble pillars covered with the cloths of black velvet; the velvet was swished away.

A sudden hush.

On each pillar was a thick, cut-glass crystal cube, and inside each cube was a piece of art.

'A miniature from the Mughal court!' whispered Mrs Pritti, the TV presenter, looking at the pillar nearest them. Ajay followed her gaze, and for a moment – his heart humming against his chest – he forgot everything. Encased in crystal on the pillar was a painting, the size of Ajay's thumb, of a Mughal queen about to fly a falcon. They looked alive! The falcon's bronze feathers seemed to glint and rustle; the queen's veil, drawn so finely in white that it seemed almost transparent, seemed to float and glisten as it wrapped itself around her in the air.

Ajay stole a glance at Yasmin, who was washed in liquid silver by the nearest spotlight. Awe and anguish mingled in her wide emerald eyes as she stared at the painting. Ajay bit his lip. She had once tried to describe how art affected her – how much its beauty hurt her.

The hush and his thoughts broke to a wave of thunderous applause.

Attendants flung the black velvet cloths back over more artwork – a glistening marble statue; a piece of exquisite embroidery picked out in stiff silver thread that blazed in the light; a whorled necklace of intricate gold – and, using tiny wheels on the bottom of the pillars, rolled them away so that they disappeared out of sight.

Ajay felt a pang in his heart then – at seeing such beauty and craftsmanship, and having it vanish before his eyes.

There was a drum roll, and on to the stage came Mrs Shania, a corrupt politician who Ajay and the team had come up against before.

'What's she doing here?' said Yasmin aghast, shaken out of her wonder.

Ajay felt bitterness fill his mouth. Mrs Shania, with a sweeping up-do and red nails, who, no matter how Ajay tried, always seemed to be able to avoid justice. She smiled at the guests. 'It honours me to be able to present the nicest billionaire in India! Mr Jhoot!'

Next to Ajay, Kai made a sound that was somewhere between a choke and a growl.

'We need to wait, Kai! The map – we need to know where it is!' Ajay whispered, his heart burning with fear. What if Mr Jhoot had already given it to someone else for safekeeping? How would he get it back for Kai then?

As Mr Jhoot stood on a stage at one side of the room, all around, discreet but visible, bodyguards stepped into place, looking lethal in their sharp-cornered suits. Ajay bit his lip.

The crowd in front of him raised and clinked their glasses, repeating: 'The nicest billionaire in India!'

Mr Jhoot smiled as Mrs Shania left the stage, and called for quiet. 'Thank you. Thank you. Welcome all. Tonight, for just a few moments, you have glimpsed some of the wonders from my Collection of Marvellous Objects. On the first of next month, they – and others – will be auctioned by the prestigious International Auction House, Crooks', at an event that I have now moved to take place in the Thar desert – an event that will be run jointly with The Big Museum in England.'

Ajay saw Kai turning red, like a hot, glowing metal kettle just about to boil over.

He felt his own skin burn. Holding on to Kai's collar as tightly as he could, his knuckles turned white.

Where was that map?

Mr Jhoot swept his eyes over the audience, and his smile became even bigger. Almost as if he couldn't help himself, he stepped forward, and the bodyguards around him, in their slick suits, shifted imperceptibly to keep formation.

'And the biggest news of all. At the Auction, for sale, will be one of the greatest treasures in the world.' Mr Jhoot's eyes went misty. 'Kept secret for centuries, it is a Treasure said to be worth more than the Koh-i-Noor. A Treasure which is valuable beyond all measure. A Treasure that will – at a stroke – make its owner the richest person in the world.'

Unconsciously, he tapped the right pocket on his jacket, and in the warm, flashing spotlight, Ajay saw the top of the metal tube reflecting the light.

The map!

Ajay held his breath. He needed to stay calm. He needed a plan to get the map back calmly, discreetly, without drawing any attention—

'MY MAP!' Kai shouted next to him.

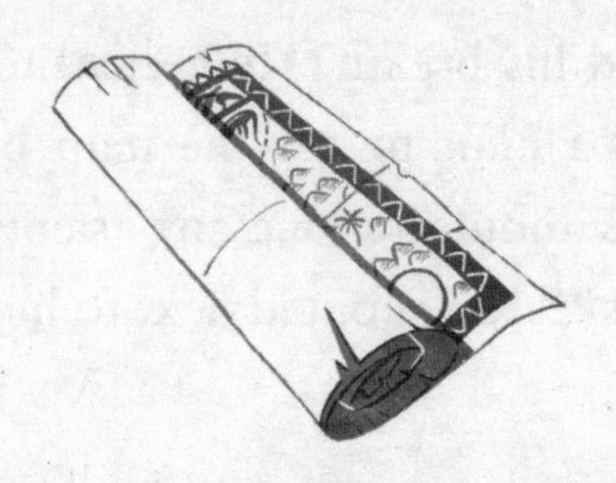

10

Ajay froze.

Kai's yell ricocheted across the crowd.

Mr Jhoot's smile dropped as one of the spotlights spun, like a lamp at a prison camp, and shone directly on to them.

Ajay, half-blinded by the beam of light, watched with streaming eyes as Mr Jhoot recovered, straightened, and spoke. Mr Jhoot's tone was one of bemused innocence, as he gently addressed Kai. 'Your map?' He turned to the rest of the crowd, his eyes sparkling. 'Honoured guests. Through the kindness of my heart, I invited these railway kids into my home. And now they claim that they own all the objects in it?'

The crowd was silent, then began to be swept with gusts of laughter.

'Priceless. Utterly priceless!' said Mrs Pritti, tapping her glass of champagne.

Ajay ignored her and stared at Mr Jhoot.

'I think,' said Mr Jhoot, shaking his head at Kai, 'that you will find that the map is *mine*.'

The billionaire's eyes were so wide, and his tone sounded so reasonable, that for a juddering split-second Ajay was filled with doubt.

'Liar! It's MY MAP!' shouted Kai. And with a tug, he burst free of Ajay's grip, dropping his suitcase to the ground.

'No – Kai!' shouted Ajay.

But Kai was barrelling forwards . . .

ducking and diving through the guests . . .

and heading straight for Mr Jhoot!

A bodyguard built like an army commander stepped down from the stage, blocked Kai's path and bent to catch and crush him.

Kai crouched and rolled like a bowling ball, spiralling through the bodyguard's legs!

Three other guards stepped out, forming a barrier between Kai and Mr Jhoot, but this time they were armed with truncheons.

'Help us!' Yasmin pleaded to the crowd, running to help Kai.

Instead of helping, Mrs Pritti blocked her path. 'What did I say? Vermin!' And then, as if a thought struck her, she smiled with sudden malice and tipped her glass of champagne over Yasmin.

A guest in a velvet suit next to Mrs Pritti gaped – then, looking thrilled, threw a second glass over Yasmin.

Ajay watched, rooted to the spot in horror, as Yasmin, spluttering and coughing, started shaking with shock. Her hair was matted – her face drenched in liquid and golden bubbles.

'That's the idea!' laughed Mrs Shania, pointing at Yasmin and Mrs Pritti from where she was standing in the crowd. 'We should hosepipe them down!'

Through the champagne dripping from her hair, Yasmin's eyes glittered.

One of the three bodyguards in front of Kai swung at him with a truncheon. Kai ducked and avoided the full force of it, but the edge caught the side of his head, causing his spectacles to fly off and land on the ground. Kai, blinking like a newborn puppy, fell on to all fours, reaching around for them. The guard stood towering above him, then slowly, deliberately, stepped on to the fallen spectacles, shattering them into shards with a horrible crunch that caused Kai to flinch.

And through it all, Mr Jhoot surveyed the scene in front of him, continuing to look relaxed, and smiled, tapping the map in his jacket pocket.

Ajay's rage exploded.

11

In fury, Ajay reached for the nearest thing to him – the cakes! He threw them (with heavy top spin!) at the bodyguard who had stepped on Kai's glasses, splattering the guard with whipped cream.

'Not the cream cakes!' he heard Saif's voice beg sadly next to him. 'They're the best . . .'

The other two bodyguards stepped forward. Ajay took two more round cream cakes in his hands and ran forwards, whirling them.

SPLAT!

SPLAT!

The bodyguards' faces filled with cream – they

stumbled – and fell!

A door opened from the side, and more guards rushed in carrying truncheons. But before they could reach Ajay, the lead saxophone player from the band surveyed what was happening, then calmly pulled up the wires to the amplifiers, causing the bodyguards to trip, and trip, and trip over each other – like dominoes.

Thank you! Ajay silently waved. The saxophone player waved back, winked, then, raising a hand, motioned to the band to

start playing – a rollicking, dancing, upbeat tune. A tune with rhythm!

Mrs Shania scooped up a plate of food next to her and hurled it at Ajay, but missed, catching an elderly guest with a distinguished white beard squarely on the nose, who in turn crouched and whirled two buns in her direction, which landed just short – straight on to two other guests who blinked, then gleefully returned fire.

Seeing Mr Jhoot trying to slip back through the crowd, Ajay yelled: 'Food fight!'

For a moment, nothing happened.

Then, guest after guest started grabbing whatever bread rolls, pastries, and samosas were nearest and throwing them at whoever they could.

Through the rain of flying food, Ajay could just see Kai spring and (more by luck than design) land on top of Mr Jhoot, and grab the map from Mr Jhoot's pocket.

As Mr Jhoot tried to tear Kai (who was clinging on like an octopus to a rock) off him, Mrs Pritti grabbed one of the truncheons that had fallen from a guard's hand and rolled towards them, and moved towards Kai.

'Oh no you don't!' blazed Yasmin, as she grabbed hold of two pink cocktail glasses and flung the sugary-sweet iced drinks over Mrs Pritti.

'Saif!' cried Ajay.

Saif, looking very aggrieved, hurriedly shoved two cream buns in either cheek, looking like a stuffed hamster. Then, squirting some engine oil that he always carried on to the wheels of the cake trolley, he put Kai's suitcase on to the bottom tray and started to push the trolley. It started slowly rolling forwards.

Ajay turned – the bodyguards were picking themselves up, wiping the cream off their faces, and looking at Ajay with bloodshot eyes.

One raised a truncheon and made for him. Desperately, Ajay threw three cream cakes with spin, but the bodyguard batted each one away with ease, and a wolf-like grin.

Cream cakes against metal truncheons!

Ajay squeezed his eyes shut.

'Ajay!' screamed Saif from behind him. Ajay's eyes snapped open. He turned and saw the huge metal trolley hurtling and clattering towards him, with a panicked Saif holding on to the handles for all he was worth.

Ajay's heart flew out of his chest.

He, the mighty editor of *The Mumbai Sun*, was about to be flattened like a crispy dosa!

But just as it was about to roll over him, the trolley screeched to the left. As it whooshed past, Saif held out his hand. Ajay grabbed it and swung forwards through the air, landing with a puff and expulsion of air on the front of the trolley. He could see the bodyguard's ferocious look replaced with stark terror as he and Saif and the trolley careened forwards out of control.

The other bodyguards dived out of the way.

Ajay felt his face turn pea-green from the speed.

In the distance, Yasmin was ducking as Mrs Pritti tried to swipe at her with a truncheon.

'Yasmin!'

The trolley was almost up to her.

Yasmin turned, blanched, and before Mrs Pritti could take another swing at her, clasped hold of Ajay's hand. A moment later, she too was on the trolley behind him.

There was just one person left.

Kai! They had to save Kai!

Ajay saw Mr Jhoot holding Kai in front of him like a kitten. Kai was flailing around blindly.

'Steer!' screamed Saif from behind him.

How?

Ajay remembered a film about the Jamaican bobsleigh team he had seen last summer, at the travelling cinema that had come to the slum!

'Lean right!' he shouted.

They all leant, and the trolley veered – just in time!

Mr Jhoot was shaking Kai ferociously until Kai's teeth chattered.

'Kai!'

Mr Jhoot, seeing the trolley racing towards him on the low stage, gasped and dropped Kai so that he landed heavily on Ajay's shoulders.

'Ow!' said Ajay, trying to peel back Kai's clammy hands from his eyes – and then shouted hurriedly, 'Left! Left!'

He twisted his head back. Mr Jhoot had recovered and was shaking his fist at them.

'Catch the thieves! They have the map!' Mr Jhoot roared from behind them.

The trolley veered towards the doors leading

out of the room.

The crowd of guests surged at them from all sides, their arms trying to pull and tug at Ajay.

In front of them, bodyguards ran to the two brass doors, putting their weight behind them to heave them shut.

The sliver of a gap between them was getting smaller and smaller.

Ajay held his breath.

The doors were closing in on them.

The last second . . .

The trolley slipped through, rolling into the corridor, and through the lift door!

The doors slammed shut behind them and they rolled off the trolley and collapsed on to the lift's floor.

They had escaped . . . with Kai's map!

12

Ajay reached up and hit the little gold buttons on the panel.

The lift dropped down, level by level, in a flurry of speed and lights.

The doors opened into the marble corridor.

The railway kids tumbled out.

Ajay looked at the dial above the lifts. A second lift was coming down after them!

'Over here!' shouted Yasmin. Ajay followed as she and the others slipped and slid like skaters across the icy marble corridor to the front door.

They landed in a crumpled heap, clambered up and together opened the front door. A moment later they ran out into the dark humid heat of

Mumbai punctuated by streetlights.

'Now what?' said Yasmin, her eyes bright in the glare of the lights.

There was a crashing behind them as if a huge group of people were rushing towards the door.

'This way!' said Ajay.

They ran along the street and could hear the crowd in a frenzy, running after them.

'I am an apprentice engineer!' Saif sobbed next to Ajay as they turned a corner. 'I am not Usain Bolt!'

'In here!' shouted Ajay, screeching to a stop and pulling back a tarpaulin that was covering the back of a fancy open-topped car.

He dropped in Kai, who was holding the map tightly to his chest. Yasmin leapt in next, followed by Saif, complaining continuously and still holding Kai's suitcase. Ajay climbed in after them, pulled the tarpaulin over them all and listened to the rush of the crowd as they ran past.

He turned to the others but couldn't make them out. Everything was pitch black.

'How long do we stay here?' whispered Kai. 'I need to keep my map safe.' Ajay caught the exhaustion underneath the words.

'Until we are safe,' whispered Yasmin comfortingly, her voice low and warm.

'A couple of hours!' said Ajay. 'We'll let the crowd search for a while. And when the coast is clear, we'll escape and go back home to the station. Right, Saif?'

No answer.

'Saif?' Ajay repeated, a little more uncertainly.

There was a hurried chomping.

Ajay grinned.

In the battle between cream cakes and truncheons, the cakes had won!

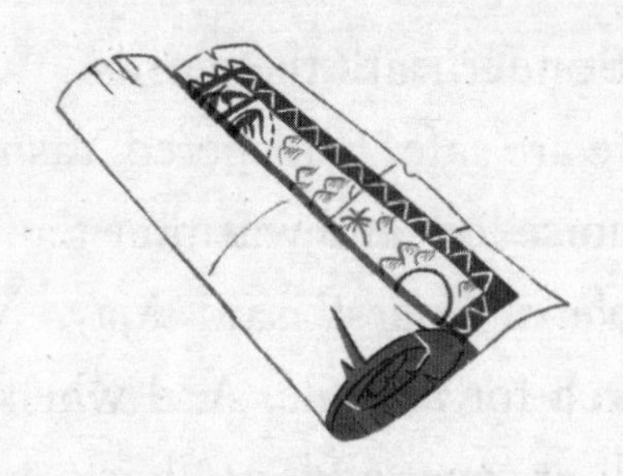

13

In the end it was a sharp dig from Saif's elbow that woke Ajay.

Ajay yawned and stretched luxuriously. It had been a very strange dream – full of ancient globes, parchment maps, and dazzling treasure. His stretched fist connected with someone's jawbone.

'Ow!' hissed Saif angrily. 'Stop that!'

Ajay sat up, wide awake. It was dim and gloomy underneath the tarpaulin, despite the spots of warm daylight that were seeping through the edge and small holes. He could see Yasmin and Kai curled up and asleep, and Saif's worried face hunched over him.

'What's happening?' Ajay asked.

'Can't you tell?' whispered Saif. 'We're on the move!'

In a panic, Ajay realized that Saif was right. The car was indeed on the move.

'We could be anywhere!' said Ajay, flailing. 'We have to get out of here!'

'And how exactly do you propose we do that?' said Saif sarcastically. 'Jump out of a moving vehicle? I am an apprentice engineer – I fix engines and build impossible machines. My muscles may be those of a superhero.' Saif pointed at his arms. 'But that does not mean that I am James Bond!'

Ajay was about to admit that he had never mistaken Saif for James Bond, when the car rolled to a halt. He and Saif looked at each other in alarm, and then at Yasmin and Kai, who were still curled next to them, fast asleep. Ajay raised his fists, whilst Saif ducked behind him and cowered. There was the sound of footsteps coming around the car, and someone saying in a British accent: 'I'll just grab the water from the back.' Suddenly, the tarpaulin was ripped away, exposing them to blazing, gold light.

Ajay's eyes watered as a figure towered over them, impossible to see in the sun's glare.

It was now or never.

He, Ajay, editor of *The Mumbai Sun*, was going to save his friends. He jumped up.

The figure whistled. 'What have we here?'

Ajay moved out of the sun's light. His heart leapt. It was the black lead saxophone player who had pulled the cord to trip up the bodyguards. Close up, Ajay noticed that the player wore a beaded bracelet in the colours of the Kenyan flag.

Ajay tried to summon up as much dignity as he could muster and pointed to his name badge, on which he had printed his title and pronouns. 'I am Ajay. Thank you for helping us at Mr Jhoot's.'

The tall saxophone player gave a warm, wry smile. 'I am Emmanuel – Emmo for short. My pronouns are he/him. You're welcome.' There was a small pause as his crinkling eyes took in the scene in front of him. 'However, now that we have done introductions, could you let me know what you are doing in the tour car?'

Ajay coughed. He was about to apologize

profusely (and explain that it was a misunderstanding, and that he and his friends were just about to get going and find a way back to the station) but was stopped by someone shouting. 'Ajay! My old friend!'

Ajay looked up and gave a cry of joy. It was Rikesh, jumping out of the driving seat and running to them at the back of the car! Rikesh – the kind rickshaw driver with a big moustache who had helped them with their space-race adventure. They clasped hands. 'Today is now like my second birthday!' Rikesh smiled broadly. 'What luck to find you here! I am driving Mr Emmanuel to his solo hotel show in Jaipur, otherwise you and I would be drinking sweet chai and swapping stories about old times.'

'You know each other?' said Emmanuel, scratching his chin in amused bewilderment.

Ajay and Rikesh nodded. Rikesh turned to Ajay. 'But Ajay, what are you and your friends doing inside this car?' And before Ajay could answer, Rikesh continued, 'I have gone up in the world, you see! After becoming the fastest rickshaw driver in Jaipur' – here he gave a nod of thanks to Saif, who waved back proudly – 'I was given the job of a driver for a chain of big hotels. I arrived in Mumbai late last night so I could collect Mr Emmanuel early this morning from Mr Jhoot's party, to drive him to his show at the most famous hotel in Jaipur.'

'Which does lead us back to my original question,' said Emmanuel patiently. 'What are you doing in the tour car?'

'We're just about to leave . . .' Ajay began apologetically.

'Coming with you to Rajasthan!' cut in Kai, who had just woken up and was forcefully pushing his way between them.

Ajay started.

Emmanuel blinked. 'I'm sorry?' he said slowly.

'Kai's right,' interrupted Yasmin coolly, before Ajay could tell Kai it was impossible. Ajay watched in shock as she stood up, her spine as straight as an arrow, fully awake and raking back her champagne-smelling hair from her eyes. She spoke directly to Emmanuel, and her voice was matter-of-fact. 'You helped us to escape Mr Jhoot. Will you help us again? We need to get to

Jodhpur. It's in Rajasthan and on your way.'

'I'm sorry . . .' began Emmanuel.

Yasmin shook her head. 'Please. You see, it's our fault that Mr Jhoot knows about Kai's map and that the Treasure of Thar is real. We have to get Kai safely to his Grandmother's, discover the secret of the map and find the Treasure before Mr Jhoot does!'

Our fault?

Ajay felt a wave of red-hot shame wash over him. It wasn't Yasmin's fault. Or Saif's. It was *his*. He was the one who had stupidly trusted Mr Jhoot and advised Kai to give Mr Jhoot the map.

He looked at the desperation in Kai's eyes, and felt sick.

Why had he convinced Kai to trust Mr Jhoot?

Emmanuel looked lost. He opened his mouth to speak but something in Yasmin's direct, trusting gaze seemed to stop him. He turned to Kai, who was glaring at him defiantly as if daring him to say no. He turned to Saif, who gave him a sorrowful look and dramatically pointed out the blisters that he had got from running away from the bodyguards. Finally, Emmanuel turned to Ajay.

It was time for Ajay to give one of his big speeches to get Emmanuel to take them to Jodhpur. They needed to warn Kai's Grandmother that Mr Jhoot now knew that the Treasure was in the south-west corner of the Thar desert. Ajay took a deep breath. He could convince anyone! But the stabbing guilt in his chest stopped him from speaking. Instead, he looked at Emmanuel and repeated what Yasmin had said – his voice broken and halting. 'You helped us once.'

Emmanuel took a deep breath and murmured slowly to himself, 'But does that mean I promise to help always?' He looked at them one by one. Then he seemed to come to a decision, nodded curtly and gave a wry smile. 'I always wanted to go on an adventure. It seems I've got one. I'll keep our pact. We go to Jodhpur together.'

Ajay felt the smallest piece of the guilt on his shoulders loosen.

There was a chance to make up for his mistake!

14

Ajay looked at the car in delight. In the bright sunshine, and free of the tarpaulin, he could see it properly: elegant and polished, a cool powdery-blue – and open-topped!

As it snaked along the dusty roads towards the highway, the warm dust-flecked wind tousled Ajay's hair and the smell of paint and oil and animals filled his nose. Squashed in between Kai and Saif dozing on one side, and Vinod, Yasmin and Jai on the other, Ajay wanted to yell with happiness at the feeling. It was as if the whole world stretched before him, full of promise and anticipation.

The Treasure of Thar – just the words thrilled him!

What a headline it would make!

And he wasn't the only one feeling the rush of joy.

Yasmin had her sketchbook out and was busy drawing the blurring, bright landscape, from time to time frowning as she used her fingers to smudge the pastel hues into shimmering blocks of colour. Jai's face shot sparks of excitement. Saif and Kai (who was wearing new glasses that Saif had fashioned for him from glass bottle bottoms ground down with sandpaper) were dozing peacefully in the shadowy corner of the back seat, and

Vinod was checking the bag he had hurriedly packed when Rikesh had doubled back to pick him and Jai up from the station.

Ajay gave a long, contented sigh as he shaded his eyes from the heated bars of gold and bronze sunlight, and the hot breeze brushed his hair. He couldn't remember ever feeling like this – the sense that time and air were flowing through his fingers. It was as if all his worries were floating away, one by one, on parachutes.

Except for one . . .

Ajay felt a cold jab of guilt through the layers of warmth at the thought of how his carelessness might have lost Kai and his Grandmother the Treasure. If Mr Jhoot had got hold of it he would have sold it at the Auction. And once sold at the Auction, the Treasure would have disappeared into a shadowy lair, perhaps abroad, never to be seen by ordinary Indians again.

Ajay shuddered.

It's all right now, Ajay reminded himself. *We'll get to Kai's Grandmother. Together we'll discover the secret of the map and the Treasure's exact location before Mr Jhoot.*

And they were making good time! In the front, Rikesh and Emmanuel were taking it in turns to play music, which had led to a mix of Bollywood beats, a rap song about heartbreak that Ajay loved and tried singing soulfully along to (until Jai said railway cats yowling were more in tune and threatened to sit on him if he didn't stop), and then jazz music like Emmanuel and his band had been playing at the party. Ajay tried to relax again and closed his eyes to the delicious slow track with sounds like a brush sweeping over drums, woven through with long, brassy notes.

Rikesh veered, then slowed down in front of a cow that had come sauntering into the car's path and was now mooing gently as if in time to the music. The car was instantly surrounded on all sides by street kids selling copies of *The Happy Paper*.

'Five rupees for The Happiest Paper you'll ever read!' shouted one.

Ajay sat up, affronted. He had forgotten about *The Happy Paper*. And now here it was, trying to cut his sales!

Rikesh was busy handing over five rupees, then

caught sight of Ajay's scowl in his mirror and had the grace to blush. 'I just like being happy,' he said lamely, quickly passing it on to Vinod.

Yasmin shook her head at Ajay. 'Leave Rikesh alone. It's called *The Happy Paper* – what harm can it do?'

'A lot,' said Vinod. His voice sounded strangled, and his hands were trembling. 'Look.'

Ajay took the paper from him and recoiled, gasping, as if the paper were a hand grenade.

On the cover, underneath a heading that read: 'Thugs and Looters on the Rampage!', was a photo of the food fight – and blown-up photos of him, Vinod, Saif, Jai, Yasmin and Kai!

15

Ajay read out the article in horror.

Yesterday evening, six dangerous looters calling themselves The Mumbai Sun *invaded the home of Mr Jhoot. Armed with round projectiles, the gang infiltrated Mr Jhoot's party and caused havoc. Damaging property and attacking innocent bystanders, the group stole a family heirloom – a map leading to the legendary Treasure of Thar – from Mr Jhoot.*

Mr Jhoot, the nicest billionaire in India, in an exclusive interview with our paper, said: 'I have worked all my life to help those in need. This gang – The Mumbai Sun *– has stolen my most precious possession. Please help me catch them!'*

Unnamed sources at the party said: 'It was terrifying. The Mumbai Sun *were like animals. We were afraid for our lives!'*

Mrs Pritti, present during the looting, tearfully described how she was trying to peacefully reason with one of the gang members when the gang member turned on her: 'The attack came out of nowhere. It was savage. If we do not hunt them down soon, I worry about where their violence will end – and what they will do with the Treasure of Thar should they track it down.'

'Peacefully reason?' said Yasmin, her fists clenched, her eyes flashing dangerously.

'Gang of six? Vinod and I weren't even there,' said Jai in disbelief.

'It's *my* map!' said Kai furiously, blinking in the sun.

'I like this photo,' offered Saif, looking at his mugshot and checking his profile and hair in the car mirror.

'Ajay,' said Vinod softly. 'What are we going to do?'

Ajay didn't answer. He was reeling with shock. 'How can it print such lies?' he whispered in a cracked voice. He couldn't breathe. He loved newspapers. He loved words; the feel of news-print on his fingers; the opening of a crisp new sheet. Newspapers were there to give voice to the vulnerable. To change the world for the better!

And now the thing that he loved above all else had been twisted like a snake. Newspapers were the one thing in the world that used to make him feel safe. How could he trust them now? What was the point in *The Mumbai Sun* if people preferred buying lies?

'Don't worry,' said Yasmin comfortingly. 'We're the team from *The Mumbai Sun*. People know us. No one will believe this rubbish.'

'I wouldn't be so sure,' said Emmanuel gently. He had taken the paper from Ajay and was quietly reading it.

Yasmin turned to him in shock, her eyes wide.

Emmanuel's voice was measured. 'People tend to believe and repeat what they read. It's easier than thinking for themselves.'

'But Mr Jhoot stole from us. *He* attacked *us*! How can *The Happy Paper* make it sound like we're the dangerous ones?'

'You'd be surprised how often that happens,' said Emmanuel drily.

'What do we do now, kind people?' said Rikesh, looking worriedly from one to another.

Ajay was looking around the road, where cars, rickshaws and cows were ambling past, and the street sellers seemed too busy to notice the resemblance of him and the others to the photos on the front page. For now, he and his friends were safe . . . but for how long?

'We keep going,' said Ajay fiercely. He was the

editor of *The Mumbai Sun*. He would do what he had always done: get the story – the true story – and print it. But first he had to make things good for Kai. 'We have to get to Kai's Grandmother and warn her that Mr Jhoot is heading to the south-west corner of the Thar desert!'

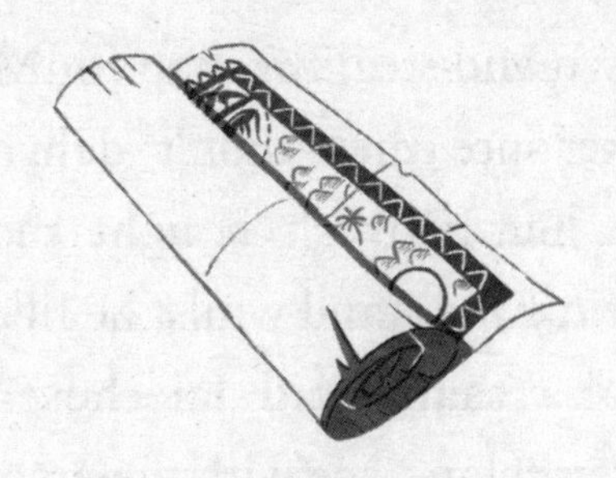

16

The cow eventually moved out of the way, and they set off again. The light was rich and dripping like hot honeycomb; the movement of the car along the highway was soothing, despite the surrounding blaring and beeping of rickshaw horns; and the music from the car speakers was relaxing and warm.

Yet Ajay's teeth were chattering. *The Happy Paper* had called them looters! How could a newspaper print such lies? They weren't looters. Mr Jhoot was! Fresh indignation washed over him, mingled with fear. What if everyone believed the lie? They could escape Mr Jhoot – but what if the whole of India decided to hunt him and his friends down and steal the map for Mr Jhoot?

To make sure they didn't dehydrate in the strobe-like heat, Rikesh bought them all fresh juices to drink at a stand whilst he filled the car up with petrol. Yasmin and Jai chose bright pink frothy watermelon juice with the pips still dancing up and down in the long glasses; Saif and Kai and Rikesh ruby-red pomegranate juice; Emmanuel and Vinod silvery-green sugarcane juice; and Ajay, his favourite – a syrupy glass of thick mango juice.

As Rikesh was waiting in line to fill the car, a little distance away, Ajay held his glass in his hand, trying to extend the moment, and hold back his fears. A gentle memory from years ago suddenly came to him – his mother finding a mango in a gutter. Starving, they had eaten the golden mango slices together, wide-eyed and laughing as the rich juice ran over their hands and faces. He would have been about the same age as Kai.

He looked to where Kai was sipping his drink and scrunching his face at the cold, sweet sharpness of his pomegranate juice.

The sound of an argument between Saif and a street kid of about the same age, with wavy pink hair and an irreverent grin, broke Ajay from his thoughts.

'Bet you can't!' said the kid.

'Bet I can!' snapped Saif, his cheeks red.

'What's going on?' said Ajay, fully attentive now.

Saif waved his hand at the kid. 'This is Ash. She thinks she can play a trick on me. I told her that I am an apprentice engineer and that it is impossible to fool me.'

'Then make a bet,' said Ash cheekily from where she was seated on the ground, her eyes impish. She flicked a coppery coin, with the sign of a falcon stamped on both sides, across her knuckles so that it gleamed in the rippling sunlight. Then she tossed it up – where it spun and flashed – caught it, and laid it on her palm. 'All you have to do is say where the coin is. Lose and I get your juice.'

'You're holding it,' said Saif, going for the glass of juice.

'Not yet!' admonished Ash. 'Once I have done this.'

She curled her hand up into a fist over the coin.

'Now?'

'Inside your fist,' Saif said confidently.

Ash opened her hand. No coin!

Saif looked stunned. He looked up and down and all around on the ground.

Ajay shook his head in disbelief. How had she done it? How had she made the coin vanish without him or Saif seeing?

'Where is it?' demanded Saif at last. 'You don't get the pomegranate juice if you've just lost it.'

'Make a fist.'

Saif scowled, but did so.

'Now open it.'

Inside Saif's hand was the coin.

Saif stared at it in silent wonder.

Ajay burst out clapping. Then he heard Mrs Pritti's silky voice coming from the radio on the juice stand. He stared at the radio and listened to the show with growing dread.

'Today's guest is Mrs Shania. And the question we will be debating today is: Are railway gangs a menace?'

'Thank you for having me here.' Mrs Shania's voice came over the radio's speakers. Ajay felt

weightless suddenly, as if the world wasn't real any more. '*And thank you for letting me share my opinion that railway gangs are not just a menace but a disease that will destroy society unless we take steps to cure it! For evidence – just look at what happened yesterday evening to Mr Jhoot, who innocently invited a railway gang into his home. I would ask ordinary citizens to be vigilant and turn in those particular thieves so that justice can be done.*'

Yasmin went pale; she turned to Ajay.

He tried to speak, but no words came out. He saw Ash sneeze and look at them all with questions in her eyes. Rikesh and Emmanuel were running back towards them, panting as they leapt into the front of the car.

'Take your time, my good friends,' said Rikesh. 'Time, after all, is a construct. But if you could possibly find it in you to construct it in a speedy manner—'

'Get in – now,' said Emmanuel, his voice strained. 'The petrol station attendant heard the radio and has got suspicious.'

'*You're* part of the railway gang that stole Mr

Jhoot's map?' said Ash, staring at them, her hand clenched around her coin.

Saif flinched.

Ajay felt ashamed. He should explain everything to her – defend himself and the team, and now *all* railway kids, against the attack in *The Happy Paper* and on the radio. He opened his mouth to speak.

Then suddenly he shut it again in a flush of anger.

Why should he have to defend himself and Saif and his friends exactly?

Ajay kept his mouth firmly shut and crossed his arms for good measure. If Ash wanted to believe the lies in *The Happy Paper*, that was all on her, not him.

Ash's eyes darkened. It was as if she could read his thoughts.

'I'll head off whoever follows as much as I can,' she said softly.

'You're helping us? Why?' asked Saif, who had not seen the interplay between her and Ajay and was eyeing her suspiciously. 'For more pomegranate juice?'

'Bullies make me sneeze,' said Ash casually,

shrugging. She got up, stood next to the car and added lightly, 'We stick together!'

Ajay and his friends piled into the car, Jai fastening a seat belt over a protesting Kai, and Rikesh turning the key to start the engine.

'I might not see you again,' said Saif suddenly to Ash. He twisted around mournfully to face her from the back seat.

Ash laughed, as the car rumbled to life. She flicked something over to Saif and, as Rikesh hit the accelerator, she shouted out: 'If you ever need me, just send me this. I'll find you.'

Saif's eyes shone.

As the car lurched and zoomed on to the road to Jaipur, leaving Ash – their new friend – far in the distance, the sun turned the pink highlights in her hair to gold. Saif picked up the object she had thrown into the car, his body still, his eyes full of wonder. Ajay looked too.

It was the copper coin, with the sign of a falcon stamped on both sides, one side with closed wings, the other open – so that when the coin was spun, the falcon seemed to fly.

17

Hours and hours later, Kai looked at Ajay over the flickering flames, and frowned, patting the suitcase next to him. 'What about getting to my Grandmother and finding the Treasure before Mr Jhoot?'

'We'll get to Jodhpur tomorrow, Kai,' said Ajay, putting on a show of confidence.

It was dark.

After driving away from the petrol station, Rikesh had cut through a side lane and landed on the red-dust ground that scattered in gold embers as the tyres tore through it. 'It will take longer, my friends, but we need to find a route off the beaten path.' The car's elegant lines gleamed as it accelerated through the roads. Kai, alert as a meerkat, had sat up, tightly hugging his suitcase with the precious treasure map inside, the wind tousling his hair, as he sat looking in the direction of Jodhpur. Eventually, with the sun dipping low in the sky creating streams of startling reds and orange, Rikesh had pulled into a patch of open, bronzed land, taken off his sunglasses and smiled tiredly at them all. 'Friends! We have been on a long journey. We rest here tonight!'

Jai and Yasmin had built a fire, and they were all sitting around it now as it crackled and snapped with apple-green-and-gold flames, and sifted up soft charcoal smoke. Vinod had already made them mugs of black, rich, hot coffee in a saucepan, which Ajay and the rest of the team were drinking in cautious, scalding sips, whilst he was taking out a bulb of garlic and an onion and ginger and spices that he had brought with him, tossing them all together with cubes of smoked paneer that charred as they hit the oil. Ajay's mouth watered.

'Let me see the treasure map . . .' he pleaded with Kai to distract himself from the smoky, delicious smells coming from the pan.

Kai shot him a look that left Ajay in no doubt that Kai might forgive but that he would never, ever forget that it was Ajay's fault that Mr Jhoot knew about the map, then – very reluctantly – gave it to him.

Ajay gulped.

He stared at the map – the lines of it, the strange symbols – and something stirred in him.

He knew nothing about his family or his past. The only things he had from it were a few scorching memories of his mother, and her pen. But here was a map, passed from generation to generation, leading to a centuries-old treasure that had survived even the British Empire's looting. Finding it *mattered*.

All they had to do was work out the secret of the map and the exact location of the Treasure, and they would find something that no one had laid eyes on for centuries. He, a railway kid, would hold in his hands something so beautiful that people would give their lives for it.

He looked up and saw Saif absorbed in trying to make the coin Ash had given him vanish, murmuring to himself something about the laws of physics. Revived by the coffee, Jai and Yasmin had got up and were playing a relaxed game of cricket in the swimming golden shadows from the fire. Vinod was patiently teaching Kai how to cook. All Ajay's friends had lost their families, or had families that had abandoned or hurt them. Only Kai still had his. Ajay looked back at the map. Was that a new coppery line that had grown across it? He shook his head – he must be more tired than he realized. He rolled Kai's map up safely, put it back into Kai's suitcase, and stared into the flickering flames.

'Something on your mind?'

Ajay hadn't even noticed that Emmanuel had stopped playing the soft, low scales he had been practising on his saxophone and had come to sit next to him.

'It's my fault,' said Ajay. And then, in a sudden burst of confidence, 'I told Kai to show Mr Jhoot the map. And now Mr Jhoot won't stop until he gets it and the exact location of the Treasure.'

Emmanuel looked pensive, stirring the embers of the fire with a stick so that they flared molten gold. 'Advice can be like a grenade. Dangerous to give and even more so to listen to,' he said at last.

Ajay looked at him miserably.

'But Ajay.' Emmanuel's voice was very gentle. 'You made a mistake. We all do from time to time. Put the mistake to one side now. All you can do is your best to make amends. You are the editor of *The Mumbai Sun*. Try to find the Treasure before Mr Jhoot and then tell the true story of the map.'

'What if nobody believes me?' said Ajay. 'What if his lies win?'

Emmanuel bit his lip. 'Ajay, as long as one person knows and speaks the truth, power, evil and cruelty *cannot* win.'

Ajay stared at him.

Emmanuel poked at the fire, setting off scattering streams of bright sparks. When he spoke again, his eyes were haunted. 'I am British. I am Kenyan. People in Britain understand the evil of concentration camps. Yet few there know or speak of the fact that the British Empire built concentration camps in Kenya, where thousands upon thousands of innocent Kikuyu people were tortured and killed – or that these concentration camps were built by the British Empire *after* the end of the Second World War. The victims of those concentration camps must never be forgotten.'

Ajay looked at him, mute with horror.

'The powerful often succeed in burying the truth but, despite all their efforts, the truth continues to exist.' Emmanuel turned to look at him. 'Find and tell the truth, Ajay. Even if it is to just one other person.'

Ajay looked at him. He wanted to cry, but couldn't.

Instead, he got up and, in the soft twilight, clasped Emmanuel's hand.

They were interrupted by a shout from Jai.

'Look!'

Ajay and Emmanuel turned to look to where Jai, his face lined with panic, was pointing in the distance.

Two pairs of headlights were racing straight towards them.

18

The hunt for Kai and his map was on.

'Get in the car!' shouted Ajay.

Saif and Vinod grabbed everyone's stuff; Emmanuel, Jai and Yasmin doused the fire; and they all jumped in. Rikesh started the car, creating clouds of sandy dust that glittered in the headlights like sharp-edged gold sequins.

The two pairs of headlights swung behind them.

Headlights belonging to two powerful and expensive sports cars.

'Buckle up, my friends,' Rikesh called back to them. He accelerated.

The cars behind them squealed closer, their hot

tires whirling red.

Ajay heard Yasmin take a sharp intake of breath; saw Saif clutch his coin and duck; and tensed as Kai looked excitedly at the twin cars, his face brightening at the thought of a race.

Rikesh tugged on the gearstick, and the car leapt forward, twice as fast.

Ajay yelled.

He could feel the ground jolting and jarring underneath – his skin was pulled tight against his face, his eyes almost blinded from the rush of wind.

He tried to open his eyes. In the side mirror he saw the two sports cars speeding up behind them.

They were coming closer and closer on either side of them in a pincer movement!

Ajay saw one sports car rush forwards, closer and bigger than the other. He raised his arm to protect his face just as the car hit them – a crash that sent him juddering and made his teeth feel as if they were coming loose from his skull. There was a fiery screech of metal and searing hot sparks, as Rikesh's car ripped across the side.

It was now skewered on the right.

Ajay – his head dizzy, his body sore from the impact – felt sparks singe his hair and skin, and cried out in pain from the burning flecks. He watched in terror, as the second car came up on the left.

'Watch out!' yelled Jai, unbuckling his seatbelt, his eyes burning a tawny fire. He jumped over the others to fight off a passenger, a shadowy form in a dark suit, who was lunging out of the first car, trying to grab hold of Kai and the suitcase.

Ajay fiercely grabbed the passenger's arm.

The passenger pulled out a bar that glinted cold and metallic in the mix of moonlight and headlights.

'Oh no, you don't!' shouted Yasmin, leaning over and whacking it out of the passenger's hand with Vinod's frying pan. Vinod was holding on to a squirming Kai, who was no longer smiling at the cars, but with fists flailing had gone to help Jai.

Jai, livid with a rare anger, bent, and with all his might shoved the other passenger back into his car.

Rikesh shook his head, as if in sorrow at the impatience of car hijackers, locked gears. He slowed down to release the car from where it had been skewered. His car dropped away on the road.

The two sports cars continued to race ahead, only seeing their mistake too late. They reversed, their tyres skidding and screeching. Rikesh hit the accelerator, his headlights bright, and headed right for them. Emmanuel gripped on to his seat.

'We're going to crash!' shouted Vinod.

Rikesh swerved his car off the road.

The two cars chasing them hit each other, locked together, and ground to a halt.

Rikesh, smiling, continued driving forwards.

Ajay twisted in the car seat, to see the drivers and passengers, wearing silvery suits, emerging from the cars, angry silhouettes against the headlights, making threatening gestures at Rikesh's car.

Ajay waved back at them.

They were free and rolling across the rocky, sandy landscape!

Yasmin pulled her hair back, with a wide smile on her face. Saif was crawling back up from where he had taken cover behind the seat, and Kai was beaming, shaking the suitcase with the map in it in glee. Jai and Vinod bumped fists. Then they all collapsed, exhausted, in the back of the car.

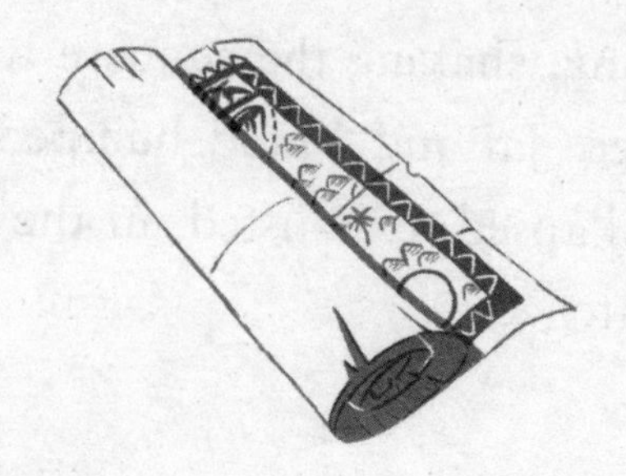

19

They got to the wall encircling Jodhpur in one piece!

The powder-blue car was too distinctive, and Emmanuel and Rikesh had to get to Jaipur – they were going to have to split up.

Saif was with Rikesh, looking at the hole in the car. 'When you are in Jaipur, get this fixed by my friend Laxmi. She is not an apprentice engineer, but she is almost—'

Yasmin glared at him.

Saif hastily corrected himself. 'She is *definitely* as good as me at repairing cars.'

Emmanuel shook the team's hands. 'A parting, not an ending.'

He and Ajay hugged.

Rikesh gave a wide smile. 'And next time we meet, I may have a truck!'

Ajay watched as Rikesh and Emmanuel got in the car.

Rikesh spun doughnuts in a farewell celebration. Then he revved the engine and with a final wave and a parting call from Emmanuel – 'I hope that you all find the treasure that you seek!' – he and Emmanuel disappeared into the distance, in a cloud of hot dust.

Ajay felt a strange ache in his heart. He had felt safe whilst Rikesh and Emmanuel were there. And now he was alone against the world.

He felt Yasmin link arms with him and breathed.

Not alone.

Yasmin, Jai, Vinod, Saif . . . and Kai.

My friends.

Kai was looking up at him, with deep longing in his eyes.

'I want to go home,' he said. 'To my Grandmother.'

Ajay put his ache aside and took Kai's hand.

He, Yasmin, Jai, Saif, Vinod and Kai turned to enter the Old City of Jodhpur.

20

Ajay's eyes widened. The Blue City!

Now that they were getting closer to his home, Kai was jumping from one foot to another in excitement. Pride was bursting from his face. Ajay understood why! Mumbai was a roaring city full of rush and ripping rhythm. Old Jodhpur was like stepping through a portal back into the past. Yet what a city it was! Just the place to start a quest!

In the distance, in the dawn light, was a soaring fort like a gold lion crouched on top of a cliff. Ajay's mouth went dry – it was powerful, impregnable, dominating – like a fortress from a story book! The old city spilt on the plains, studded with cool, cobalt-plastered buildings which reflected the sun's slanting clear light in a misty blue haze. As they walked through the old city, through a maze of bazaars, Kai's voice took on the solemn intonation of the wildlife presenter again. 'Jodhpur used to be one of India's main trading outposts. In the sixteenth century it was on the route to Central Asia. Grandmother told me there would have been caravans here selling ivory, salt and camels!'

Ajay was tripping over himself as he turned this way and that, his attention caught by the sparkle of the stalls. It was not hard to imagine the city as it had been centuries ago – a plucky, vibrant outpost carved out of the rocky landscape.

'It's so beautiful!' Yasmin was glowing with excitement. She picked up some bright juttis that had been fashioned by a cobbler sitting cross-legged on the side of the street.

'Look at this!' she said, trying one on and admiring her reflection in the mirror.

Further on, a sweet seller, tired and sweat-damp, was whisking a huge metal bowl filled with boiling milk and sugar over a charcoal fire. With his last rupees, Ajay bought a tray full to the brim of doodh laddu that was tipped for him and his friends into brown paper bags.

As they followed Kai on the last stretch of road to his Grandmother's home, Ajay felt his spirits lift. Everything was better on a full stomach of creamy milk-flavoured sweets! They would get to Kai's Grandmother's, Ajay decided, and with her help find the exact location of the Treasure, defeat Mr Jhoot, and make all their dreams real.

They were the team from *The Mumbai Sun*!

Of course they would win!

Kai was rushing ahead, leading them on a road that went past a show with puppets enacting a battle scene. The puppets, with their carved and painted wooden heads and silky clothes, were fiery and beautiful in the light of the twin burning torches that framed the stage. And the story was one that Ajay loved – full of glory, and sacrifice and honour. Yasmin, Jai, Vinod, Saif and Kai's mouths dropped open, mesmerized by the mastery of the puppet master.

An old copy of *The Happy Paper*, stained with oil from food, caught Ajay's eye as it fluttered from where it had been caught on the roof of a food stall, punctured his good mood. Its headline: 'Mr Jhoot seeks help to catch looters!'

A puppet master pulling at people's strings.

Disquiet filled him, like a tiger treading over his shadow.

Mr Jhoot won't stop until he has Kai's Treasure.

Ajay felt terror seep into him with a sudden, precise knowledge of the truth.

Mr Jhoot won't stop for anything.

Ajay herded the others back to the path to find Kai's Grandmother's house, trying to stop them from seeing his worry. Was that a shadow following them, or his imagination? He was concentrating so hard that it was only suddenly that he realized they had turned a corner and stopped.

'Grandmother!' cried Kai, rushing towards a small shack with an open doorway. 'I'm back. And I have fetched Guardians to help!'

They had brought Kai home!

21

A few hours later, they were all sitting in Kai's Grandmother's home, safe and sound, drinking mugs of warm milk flavoured with chopped pistachios and almonds, spicy crushed cardamom, sugar and golden strands of saffron, as Kai regaled her with his adventures.

'. . . and that was the end of the car chase! I was very brave,' he added for good measure.

Kai's Grandmother nodded. Her hair rippled to her shoulders in waves. *She holds herself like a queen*, thought Ajay. 'I'm sure you were,' she replied, ruffling his hair, but there were traces of anxiety in her dark eyes and across her delicate features.

Ajay took a deep gulp of the sweet milk to steady himself. 'It was my fault that Mr Jhoot found out about the map and where in the Thar desert he can find the Treasure.'

'All his fault,' added Kai, nodding in agreement.

Kai's Grandmother shook her head. 'If Mr Jhoot heads the organization of the Four Snakes, he has been searching for the map for decades. With his resources, it was only a matter of time before he found it.' She looked at each of them in turn, as if taking their measure. 'The question is, what we do next?'

'Destroy the map,' said Jai unexpectedly. At the shocked looks from the others, he shrugged. 'Isn't it obvious? If the map is destroyed, the Treasure can stay hidden in the desert and no one will ever know about it. It will be safe for ever.'

They all went quiet. Ajay found himself rebelling at the idea. There were so many Indian treasures stolen and kept far across the ocean in British museums that railway, street and slum kids in India would never see. But here was one that he could find and save – something so marvellous, that a glimpse of it might change their lives.

'No,' Yasmin said quietly. 'Don't you see? The Guardians – the people who were charged with protecting the Treasure from the British – must have meant for the Treasure to eventually be found. Beautiful things aren't meant to be hidden away – they are meant to be shared.'

'And the Treasure *won't* stay hidden for ever,' said Vinod decisively. 'Given enough time, Mr Jhoot is rich enough to dig under the whole of the south-west corner of the desert if he wants to. If we don't destroy the map, Mr Jhoot will chase us until he gets it. After all, the Auction is in less than a week and the quickest way to get the Treasure is to steal the map from us. But if we destroy the map, he'll find the Treasure on his own and sell it anyway – and it will be all our fault!'

Ajay's mouth dried up.

'We have to keep the map and find the Treasure first,' said Yasmin.

Ajay looked around at his friends' faces and was suddenly hit by the enormity of what they were agreeing to do. They were railway kids, not desert kids!

(Although perhaps they were *dessert* kids . . .)

'We should go now,' agreed Kai, scrambling down.

'Wait, Kai!' said his Grandmother. She opened up the map that Kai had given her and put two paperweights – rocks with coloured quartz – on either side. 'We need to find the Treasure's exact location. And the Guardians who came before us won't have left the Treasure unprotected. There will be trials – and you'll need keys to solve them.' In a tone of infinite regret, she continued softly, 'I knew the secrets of the map once, but I thought it was safer not to act on the knowledge and to leave the Treasure hidden . . . and then my memory started to fragment.'

She frowned suddenly and gave a sharp intake of breath.

Tracing the faint line that had appeared when Ajay had last looked at the map, she asked urgently: 'This copper line – has it always been here?'

Ajay felt embarrassed. 'I saw it when I was sitting by the fire just before the car chase. I thought I was imagining it.'

Kai's Grandmother looked at him in startled

excitement. Her hand hovered over the map in hope. 'Perhaps . . .' she whispered. 'Perhaps I've not forgotten everything after all.'

She took a deep breath. Then, taking a match-stick from a box, she struck it against the side of the box. It scraped and, with a sizzle and flare, lit, smelling of fire and soot. She carefully waved it underneath the paper.

Kai shot out of his seat, his eyes full of terror; Yasmin was not far behind. But the flame was far enough away for the map not to crackle and fall into ashes.

Ajay gasped. A hidden line was appearing and spreading on the map. As he watched Kai's Grandmother passing the flame back and forth, the coppery line became clearer and darker and spread like a wire across the map – the route the Guardians wanted the finders of the map to take from Jaisalmer Fort to the desert. All Ajay and his friends now had to do was follow it!

But the secret route wasn't the only thing that was appearing on the map. Next to the red cross appeared a drawing of an oasis fringed with trees and, a little way past it, an image of a pillar. Clues to the exact location of the Treasure!

Ajay's blood thrummed and happiness flooded through him, making him feel like he was lit from inside.

'There was always the danger of the map falling into the wrong hands. The Guardians took precautions.' Kai's Grandmother looked like a young girl, brimming with adventure. She turned to look at them each in turn, her eyes searching. 'If you find the oasis, the Treasure will be close by. I have a friend who lives in the desert. He may agree to help you locate it. And see the path revealed by the flame?' Ajay and the others nodded. 'You must go along it,' she traced the coppery path with her finger, 'and stop off at these two points!' She pointed at the rest stops, one of which was near an outcrop of land.

'Why?' asked Saif, intrigued.

Kai's Grandmother's brow furrowed in concentration. But then she shook her head. 'I . . . I can't remember. I had even forgotten about the secret to unlocking the map until Ajay reminded me.' She turned to them, and in her regal face Ajay could see knots of tension and hidden strain. 'I am a

Professor of Geology, but I'm forgetting things – fragments – some small, some big. My memory is like a piece of lace with tears and holes and, as much as I try, I can't stitch it back together again. I think it is getting worse.'

She took a deep breath, her face creased in pain and shattered sadness. Kai stood up and hugged her.

'I'm sorry,' she whispered. 'As much as I try, I can't remember more than I've told you. And you may be at risk because of it.'

'It's OK,' said Ajay comfortingly. He made his words into a promise. 'We'll find the Treasure.'

Kai's Grandmother's eyes sparkled, and for a moment it felt as if she would be able to throw off the physical frailty that kept her seated, like a shawl. When she couldn't, there was a look of frustration in her eyes. But when she spoke, it was with authority and warmth.

'Are you sure? You'll be in danger.'

Ajay, Vinod, Jai and Yasmin nodded. Saif looked like he was still trying to decide. 'What sort of danger exactly?' he said nervously. 'I want to make an informed decision.'

'I'm going too!' said Kai.

'Oh no you're not,' said his Grandmother, the set of her mouth exactly like his. Ajay could see where Kai got his stubbornness from! 'Kai, listen to me – you're too young. You've already gone on one dangerous mission to get help. You've now completed that mission. Ajay and his friends can – if they are willing – do the rest.'

Kai looked at her mutinously.

Ajay was surprised that he felt a strange feeling in his chest at the idea of Kai not being with them any more. A sort of ache and warmth at the same time.

Heartburn from drinking too much milk! Ajay decided.

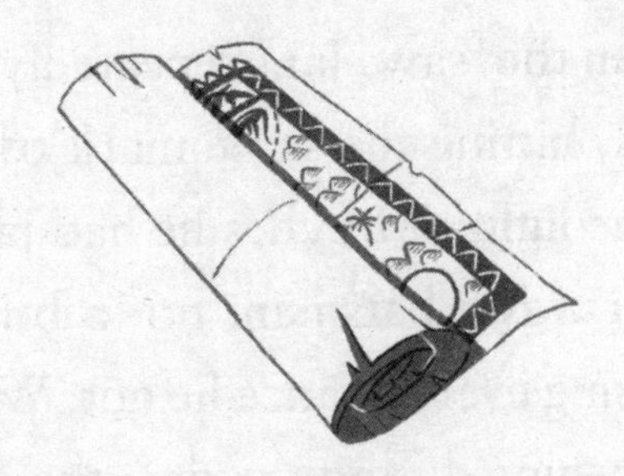

22

Ajay couldn't sleep. He was plagued by images of flying copies of *The Happy Paper*. He woke up in a cold sweat. He was Ajay, editor of *The Mumbai Sun*! He had faced down powerful enemies before, so why was he so afraid now?

Because The Happy Paper *is making everyone hate me.*

And I don't want to be hated.

He got up as quietly as he could, stepped over a snoring Saif, and went out into the hot, spice-scented night air. There was a rich blood moon in the sky, and unexpectedly he thought of their friend, the astronaut Anita, and waved, just in case she might see it from where she was.

And then he saw Jai, repeatedly bowling a cricket ball, hitting the same mark over and over again by the light of torches he had placed on the ground. Jai was a batsman, not a bowler, but he was practising every chance he got. With the blazing hot sunshine during the day, the only time he could play cricket these days was in the cool hours at night. Quietly, Ajay took over bowling so that Jai could bat, and for a while they played back and forth in silent companionship, the rhythm of bowling and batting taking over.

'Do you think people can forget the past?' Jai asked, leaning forward to bat one of the balls into the side of the courtyard. The question was unexpected – a curveball. Something in the intensity of it made Ajay pause.

'I don't know,' Ajay said.

The space filled between them.

Ajay ran to pick up the ball, to cover his emotions. *I can't remember*, Kai's Grandmother had said. What if he, Ajay, forgot his mother?

Was it a mango they had found in the gutter and eaten together? Or a sweet custard apple? Already, he wasn't quite sure.

He wished he had just one photo, to remind him what she looked like.

Seeing Kai with his Grandmother had dredged up old memories like fishes that glinted and spun in silver, but which he could only see bits of here and there. Ajay couldn't see the whole thing. The only thing that stopped his mother from evaporating altogether was her fountain pen. It was real. It was something he could hold on to, to remind him that *she* had been real too.

His thoughts were broken by Jai's murmur behind him.

'I wish I could,' said Jai. 'Forget, I mean.'

Ajay started. 'But why . . .' He stopped.

All railway kids had something in their past that hurt to remember. Sometimes, late at night, one or another would gasp or cry out in pain.

Not Jai.

But Ajay had seen Jai's clammy terror when they walked past a police station; the longing in his golden eyes when he saw Ajay, Vinod, Yasmin and Saif laughing together on the steps of the railway station; the way he sometimes looked at them all as if he was terrified that they would disappear.

What happened to you, Jai? And what can I say to help?

'The past can't hurt you,' Ajay said at last, his words stirring the dark.

'How can you be so sure?' said Jai, whacking the ball.

'Because it's true,' Ajay said confidently.

When Jai looked unconvinced, Ajay thought for a moment, then got a stick and started sketching on the ground. 'Look! People are like doughnuts! Mr Jhoot, for instance. He seems like a nice sugary, fried doughnut all the way through.' Ajay drew what he thought was a good impression of a doughnut. 'But when he's squashed, instead of nice custard or jam, all that comes out is lies. You've been squashed lots of times, Jai. And every time you look out for us all! You're a sportsperson all the way through. *The past can't hurt someone like you.*'

Jai looked at him uncertainly.

'You're a sportsperson like Muhammad Ali!'

Jai stared in front of him, and Ajay could see the vein in his throat pulsing.

'Don't you see, Jai?' Ajay tried again, desperately.

'You're the best! The Greatest Of All Time!'

Something in Jai's expression shifted.

'And my friend,' Ajay added simply.

Ajay saw Jai's face flush with warmth. And then he murmured, 'A G.O.A.T? Me?'

He shook his head at Ajay's confidence.

Ajay didn't understand why Jai was shaking his head. He should see himself the way Ajay saw him! Then he would never lack confidence!

Jai looked at him and his golden eyes went wide. Ajay held his breath.

Jai's shoulders softened. He smiled. And the memories that were haunting him were beaten back – at least for now.

They turned to go inside. Just before they did, Jai, with a sudden flash of exuberance, flung the cricket ball up and whacked it with his bat. It spun in the sky with the promise of a shooting star.

23

They were on a truck to Jaisalmer. Ajay sneezed. The five of them had stowed away among lots of hay and sweet-smelling straw that was being transported there.

Ajay had said goodbye to Kai and his Grandmother at their home, expecting more of a protest from Kai. But Kai had given him his suitcase quickly and run off, leaving Ajay with that strange sensation of heartburn again.

Kai's Grandmother had taken him to one side and spoken one last time. 'Ajay, those that steal and hold on to other people's past don't just steal goods – art, jewels, statues – they steal people and countries' identities. *You must find the secret of the Treasure before Mr Jhoot!'*

Ajay held his mother's pen tightly. He would do everything in his power to fulfil the quest!

'I miss Kai,' said Yasmin, out of the blue, as the truck rumbled on.

Ajay frowned. He did too, but would not admit to it. 'I do not,' he said grandly. 'Kai is irritating and very stubborn!'

Jai looked up, his gold eyes dancing. 'Like someone else we know?'

Ajay ignored him. 'Perhaps when he grows up, he will be more responsible,' he continued magnanimously. 'But he only would have slowed us down now.'

There was a splutter amongst the straw.

Ajay, Jai, Vinod, Yasmin and Saif looked at each other.

Jai put his hand into the straw, as if it were a lucky dip, and picked up Kai by the scruff of his neck. Kai did not look guilty. His arms were crossed, and he was spluttering through the blanket of straw covering him. 'How dare you call me stubborn!'

The others looked at him aghast.

'What are you doing here?' said Vinod.

'Your Grandmother will be so worried!' said Yasmin, her brows drawn together.

'I've left her a note,' Kai informed them. 'She will understand.' He grabbed the suitcase. 'This is *my* quest.'

Jai was the first of them to recover. 'Ajay, what are we going to do?' he said, his voice low with worry. 'We can't get out of the truck until we reach Jaisalmer, and even then we can't send Kai back on his own!'

Ajay was furious.

Of all the stupid, reckless . . .

He glared at Kai, who was scrunching up his nose.

What were they going to do? Jai was right. There was no way of getting Kai back safely.

Ajay thought through all the possibilities and scowled.

'He stays with us,' Ajay said at last, seeing no other way out.

His temper was not improved by Kai sitting back in the straw, smiling sunnily at him.

24

Jai stood looking at Ajay on the roof of Jaisalmer Fort. 'So, to get things clear, we have less than a week to unlock the secrets of a treasure map, find treasure that has been hidden for centuries – and may or may not still exist – in the middle of a *desert*?'

Ajay nodded. They were in a race with Mr Jhoot – they had to find the Treasure first!

Jai pushed his hand through his hair, lost for words. Vinod, Saif and Yasmin looked at each other. Kai jumped up and down. Ajay had rung Jodhpur railway station from the fort and sent a message to Kai's Grandmother. He hoped that she would understand.

Ajay looked down from the highest point of the fort. Jaisalmer, the Desert City, unfurled before them like a copper carpet, each unique building looking in the glowing sunlight as if it had been stitched in gold. Ajay rubbed his eyes and shivered in the hot-sparked heat. He had never seen a city more beautiful. It rose up against the sands. Some buildings were made of sandstone, intricately carved, throwing dancing patterns of shadows on to the roads thronged with people. And, in the distance, he could just make out a glimpse of the ochre and copper tints of the great shifting dunes beyond.

The Thar desert.

He had seen deserts in films. None of them had prepared him for the vast wonder he was catching a glimpse of now.

Ajay broke from his reverie. 'Kai, can we look at the map?'

He had decided to, with the self-restraint that came from being older, good-heartedly forgive Kai.

Kai (totally unaware of Ajay's good-hearted nature) took the map out of his suitcase and, setting it on a pillar, they pored over it in the sun's light.

'Here's the fort,' said Ajay, pointing. 'And the

red cross for the Treasure.'

'And here's the path to the cross,' said Yasmin, tracing it delicately with her finger just as Kai's Grandmother had.

'Which means the first stop to get to the Treasure is here!' said Saif.

His face looked befuddled.

'That can't be right! It's the middle of the only lake in Jaisalmer.'

Vinod looked at where he was pointing. 'I think it is – the right spot, I mean,' he said quietly. 'And if it is, we're going to need supplies: food to take us all the way to the Thar desert, rope (you should always travel with some rope) . . . and fishing rods to trawl the lake in case the Treasure is under water!'

Ajay nodded. It was time for the editor of *The Mumbai Sun* to take charge!

'Jai, Yasmin – find a way of getting to the lake,' Ajay ordered. 'Saif – get the rope and fishing rods; Vinod, Kai and I will go to get food to sustain us. We meet back at the fort this evening.'

The Quest for the Treasure of Thar was underway!

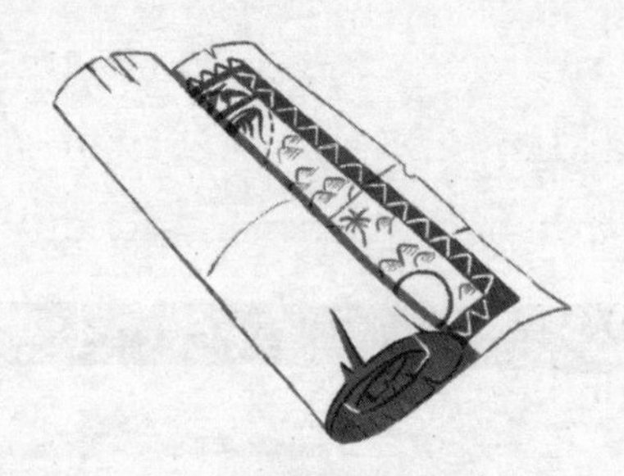

25

Ajay sniffed the air hungrily. If they were going to follow the route on the map, they needed food supplies – and this was the perfect place to get them! Trails of pungent smells enticed and beckoned as he and Kai followed Vinod through wide sand-filled streets. Vinod walked as if in a dream. As he breathed in the scent of cloves, sifted through dried red chillies and watched spice masters weigh and grind secret combinations of nutmeg, cardamom and warm cinnamon, happiness mingled with determination on his face.

'Ajay! Kai! Look around! Look at all the spices. Can you imagine what I could do with this saffron? I could cut chunks of mango and stir them into saffron-scented milk and sugar! Or with this cardamom? I could stir it with clarified butter and crushed almonds and milk to make a sweet hot syrup.'

Kai nodded furiously.

Ajay too felt his stomach rumble. He liked it when Vinod got inspired – it meant lots of tasty new recipes!

Still, they had to hurry if they were going to find the Treasure. If the Auction was in five days' time, Mr Jhoot would not be far behind them, doing everything in his considerable power to find it too.

Seeing that a forklift truck was not going to get Vinod to move from the spice market before he was ready, Ajay said, 'Meet us back at the fort. I'll go with Kai and see if Saif needs any help finding supplies.' He might as well have been a desert breeze for all the notice Vinod took of him.

Ajay took Kai by the hand. The two of them ran up and down the sparkling market. Ajay stopped short. A copy of *The Happy Paper* was floating around with the headline: 'Railway Kids: These so-called victims must be caught!'. Ajay felt sick. So *The Happy Paper* was not just sold in Mumbai? It was a national newspaper?

Does all of India hate railway kids now?

'Where is Saif?' said Kai at last, his large eyes full of puzzlement.

And then they spotted Saif – coming out of a bookshop! He looked guilty when he saw Ajay and Kai, hurriedly hiding the packages he had bought behind him.

'What's that?' said Ajay, curiosity winning over annoyance. Saif only had enough money from sales of *The Mumbai Sun* to cover buying equipment for their quest. What was he doing in a bookshop?

Saif coughed. Then spoke as if he had prepared a long speech. 'Don't worry, I've done what you asked. I ordered and paid for all the supplies we need – it used up everything except for three rupees!' He fished in his pocket and gave three rupees back to Ajay. 'But I had some time to kill, so I fixed the shop's cash machine – and in return they gave me this . . .'

From behind his back, he produced with a flourish a second-hand book, which he proudly showed to Ajay and Kai. The book had tattered covers and ink-black illustrations: 'Ten Steps to Being a Miraculous Magician!'

Kai looked impressed.

'But you can't be a magician! You're an apprentice engineer!' Ajay said thoughtlessly.

'That was the past!' Saif snapped back, waving his hand. 'Who cares about that? This is my future! I will be an apprentice engineer *and* an apprentice magician!'

Ajay felt contrite. He fished around in his pocket, brought out a pack of playing cards he'd found at the railway station and handed them to Saif by way of an apology. 'I think some of them are missing, but it's almost a whole pack!'

Saif accepted the apology with good grace. 'I can already show you a card trick I've learnt from chapter two!' he said, juggling the book in one hand and fanning out the cards in the other. Ajay was just about to choose one when the flicker of a reflection in the shop mirror caught his eye.

A group of people, stealthily coming towards them.

Despite the heat, they were wearing sleek suits,

as they had in the car that had chased them, and were carrying truncheons.

Ajay rubbed his eyes to be sure.

One spotted them, pointed at Kai's suitcase, and shouted 'Get him!'

Mr Jhoot's bodyguards. They were after Kai's treasure map!

Ajay grabbed Kai's arm and called to Saif.

'Run!'

26

They ran.

They raced through the honeycombed streets, ducking past a silver jewellery stand. The jeweller spun like a Catherine wheel, and the necklaces he was carrying chimed like a hundred tinkling bells. The bodyguards ran after them. Ajay could hear their boots stomping behind them.

'This way!' He tugged at Kai's arm, pulling him and his suitcase through a street full of sari sellers.

'Which way?' panted Saif behind them, hugging his book. 'I am an apprentice engineer, not a—'

His words were muffled, as he got caught up in

sheets of pink and turquoise that wound around and around and around him, so that he looked like a belly dancer.

'Ajay, help!' The words were indistinct.

Ajay let go of Kai's arm and ran back. A fluttering silver sari fell across his eyes, blinding him. He pulled it away with one hand, and with the other he caught one end of the turquoise sari that was wound about Saif. He tugged it like the string of a yo-yo and Saif came whirling out.

The bodyguards were thundering in their direction, towards Kai, who was now standing alone with his arms wrapped around his suitcase like a rabbit in an avalanche.

Ajay had to do something!

He reached up to pull on one of the ropes that wound in zigzags above the street, on which hung an array of rainbow-coloured saris.

'Hey! What are you doing?' cried the seller.

'I'm so sorry about my friend.' Saif stopped to apologize. 'I have been telling him that—'

'Watch out!' cried Ajay.

The rope dropped and the rainbow saris fell, creating a waterfall of material that unfurled and spilt like coloured ink down the street.

The bodyguards ran forward. Some slipped, some stumbled, others slashed their way through, but not before Ajay had taken hold of Kai's arm and dragged him to where Saif was waving.

'Ajay, through here.' Saif pointed to a hole in one of the walls. He fell on all fours and squeezed his way through. Ajay pushed Kai in, and then followed. Halfway through the hole, he looked up. A mistake.

Some of the bodyguards were running up the walls, across the roofs, trying to cut them off.

Ajay felt indignant. Where had Mr Jhoot got these bodyguards that could do parkour? The circus?

He pushed his way out of the hole and stood up . . .

Only to feel his legs rugby tackled from underneath him. He fell to the ground, every bone in his body hammering. The bodyguard, with a jutting jaw, raised a truncheon—

Ajay cowered as he saw the metal coming towards him.

Through the spaces in his hand he saw a cow bell from a stall, spinning from Kai's direction, hitting the bodyguard smack on the forehead.

CLANG!!!!!!

Ajay could practically see the birds tweeting around the bodyguard's head! He used his elbows to claw his way out and grabbed Kai's hand.

On they ran.

Saif was panting. 'Which way now? There are too many guards!'

Ajay stumbled backwards, still holding on to

Kai with one hand and grabbing Saif with the other, through expensive tortoiseshell-inlaid doors. The doors swung to and fro, giving Ajay a glimpse of the flitting shadows of the bodyguards in their shiny grey suits, as they moved as one, like silver soldiers, through the streets.

'It's OK. I think we've lost them,' said Ajay, peering through the gap.

'Ajay.' Saif was tapping on his shoulder.

'If we just give it a little bit more time, they'll be gone and—'

'Ajay!'

'—we'll be able to get back to the Fort and—'

'Ajay!' shouted Saif.

'What?' said Ajay, whirling around. 'Oh.'

They were in a large room, with mirrors on all the walls. In front of him, facing the door, was a group of very expensively dressed people, chattering in different languages, staring at them.

On top of a podium, the instructor, wearing a name tag that said 'Maya (she/her)' and dressed in slacks and ropes of beads, stepped forward smiling in a way that didn't quite mask the irritation underneath.

Her voice was piercing. 'The yoga class has started and, as we all know, punctuality is a sign of character! Please take your places at once.'

27

Ajay and Saif and Kai stared at Maya and the group in front of them.

'I think that there must be some mistake,' Ajay hurriedly explained. 'We . . .'

Saif grabbed his arm and pointed out of the door agitatedly. The shadows of the bodyguards were whirling back like a storm of bats. They hadn't been fooled.

Ajay turned back to the group. '. . . are very honoured to be here!'

One of the class, with smooth white hair, a white moustache and a distinguished manner, said politely in a British accent that sounded like double cream, 'Aren't you all a bit . . .' The tourist coughed, obviously embarrassed about breaking any rules of propriety. 'Well, you know, *young* to be in the seniors' group?'

'Oh, we're not,' said Saif immediately. 'We do so much yoga we just all *look* young!'

Ajay could hear shouts and cries from outside the door as the bodyguards started crashing through the neighbouring properties. It wouldn't be long before they came to search this one.

'We will begin by learning how to breathe,' said Maya, ignoring it all.

'Don't you know how to already?' interjected Kai in shock.

'First, clear your mind . . .'

'What if you can't?' questioned Saif, looking genuinely puzzled. 'I am an apprentice engineer and apprentice magician. I have many, many things to think about – like samosas,' he said abruptly. He licked his lips, as if a giant samosa-shaped thought had just come to him.

Ajay huffed and puffed noisily.

The whirling and crashing outside was coming closer.

'And now we go into Downward Dog,' continued

Maya serenely.

Ajay snapped back up in shock. *What?*

The class bent over and calmly put their hands on the floor at the end of the yoga mats in front of them.

Saif shrugged and started to copy the triangle shape, his eyes still misty at the thought of samosas.

The crashing was coming closer by the second. Ajay saw Kai tighten his grip on his suitcase. The bodyguards would be in any minute. He had to do something!

'Excuse me!' Ajay waved.

'What now?' Maya snapped, turning in his direction. She recovered, and gave a look of benign patience. 'I mean, how is it that I may help you to achieve a state of deep contentment and spirituality?'

'We should do the Lion pose,' Ajay improvised.

'Lion pose? Never heard of it.'

'It's very advanced,' said Ajay. 'When anyone new comes into a class, you have to look at them and do this.' He dropped into a crouching position, and let loose a full-bellied roar.

'I don't think—' said Maya.

'We should try it!' said the distinguished-looking tourist.

The bodyguards stormed in, their truncheons raised.

The whole class (apart from Maya) turned to face them, crouched and let out a huge . . .

ROAR!!!!

The bodyguards, faced with fifty people crouched and roaring at them, stopped dead in their tracks.

'Advance!' shouted Ajay.

The class started to step forward.

The bodyguards looked at each other.

'The Hedgehog pose!' Ajay improvised.

'I don't know that one either!' Maya cried plaintively.

'Curl up,' Ajay continued, 'and roll towards them!'

The class dropped down, curled, and started rolling like canonballs towards the bodyguards.

The bodyguards had no chance!

They ran, falling like skittles over the rolling human canonballs and each other, as they rushed towards the door!

Finally, seeing the last bodyguard toppled over, Ajay shouted: 'Stop!'

They stopped.

The bodyguards were left in a heap, dizzy on the floor.

'And uncurl!'

The class did so with huge smiles on their faces.

'Wonderful!' said the distinguished tourist, getting up and stretching. 'I haven't had so much fun in years!'

Maya stood over the bodyguards, her hands on her hips. 'I do tell people that they must not come into class late,' she said sternly.

The bodyguards, still dizzy, looked cowed by her imperious tone.

The class clapped enthusiastically.

Ajay, Kai and Saif took their chance to escape. Just before they whisked past the door, Ajay turned and waved goodbye.

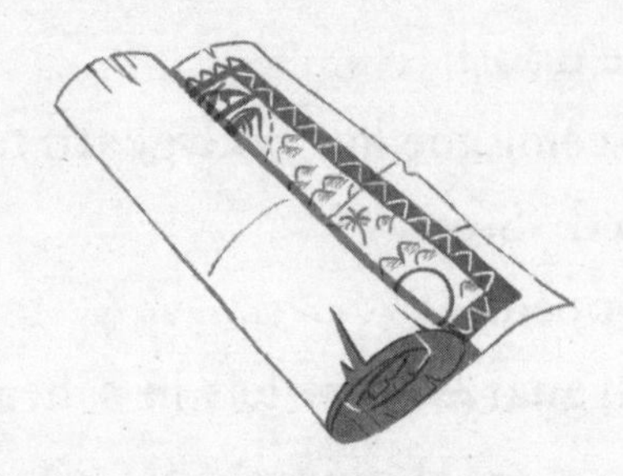

28

It was dawn. The light, as Ajay and his friends walked to Gadisar Lake, the first stop on the secret path revealed on the treasure map, was like champagne – cool and clear.

Saif was not pleased. 'Apprentice engineers (and magicians) need an optimum amount of sleep,' he said, huffing with the weight of the fishing rod and rope he was carrying as they walked through the maze of streets.

Ajay threw him a look of sympathy. Mornings were usually hard, but unlike Saif today Ajay was fizzing with energy like a shaken can of Thums Up. Now that he had escaped from Mr Jhoot's bodyguards, he could practically feel the story for

The Mumbai Sun leaping out of his fingers and on to his notebook. He held tightly on to his mother's pen as he walked eagerly past the antique dealers just setting up their stalls of bronze and green coins; and then past the hat sellers, who were draping concoctions of wound rainbow-coloured silk on to hat stands. He reached the others, who were slightly ahead of him and standing in awe in front of the massive, arching sandstone gate that led to the lake. It towered above them, encrusted with carvings, like a gateway to another world where the Treasure was there waiting for them!

They stood beneath it for several minutes. Yasmin's skirts flared as she looked up, reaching as if she wanted to touch the designs that arced above her fingertips.

'There's the lake on the map!' shouted Kai, jumping up and down, running forward.

Ajay looked out. His eyes had got used to the burning heat and dust, and to suddenly see the cool expanse of water stretching out before him, with the light glistening off it, made him feel as if the world was full of possibility and freshness.

'Let's go!' shouted Kai, running up to the lake. He stopped in his tracks, then slowly turned to the others. 'How are we getting across to the spot marked on the map?'

They all looked at each other.

Stopped at the first hurdle!

It was an hour later that Jai was able to row them steadily across the milky lake, the oars splashing through the water, causing droplets to catch and fragment in the

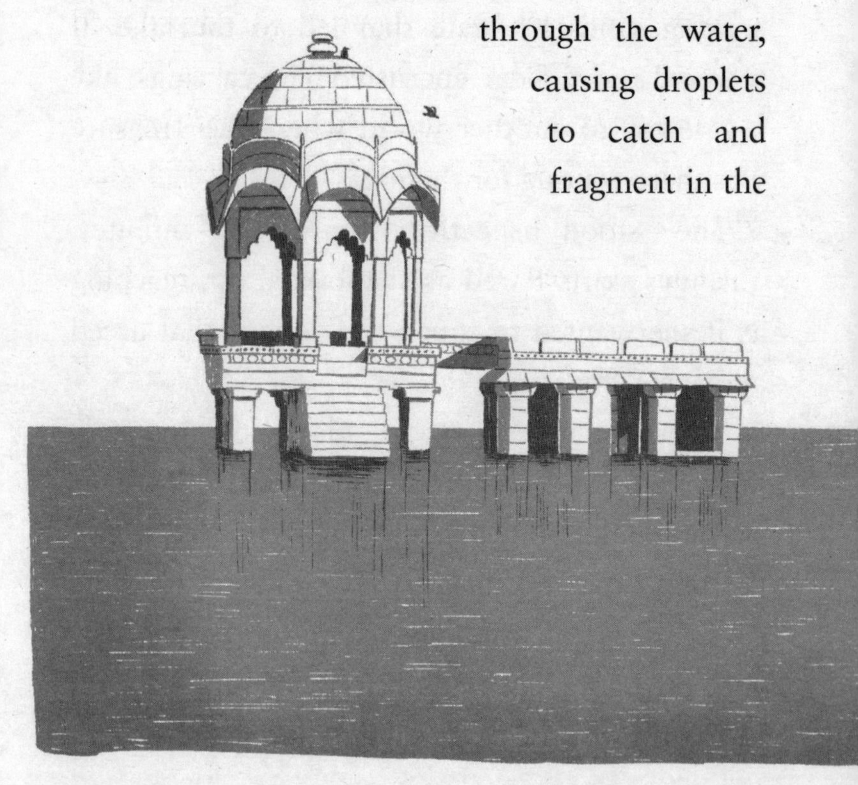

light like fluttering golden butterflies.

'Nice of the owner to lend us the boat for the day in return for an autograph from the Mumbai Cricketer,' said Yasmin, smiling at him.

Jai blushed, looking down shyly, and kept rowing forwards.

Saif and Kai were gazing ahead to find the first point on the route they had traced along the map – the middle of the lake.

Ajay leant back in the boat, his head propped up by his arm. Moving differently – first in the car, now in the boat – made his thoughts go at a different pace. He felt as relaxed and energized as a fish.

He let his eyes unfocus, and the blue-gold light

against the water and the gentle splish-splash of the oars unwind and unravel his worries. Growing up by the railway clock, he usually knew what time it was to the minute – it was a special superpower! It was so rare that he felt like this – alert, yet relaxed, as if he had dissolved and was just part of a vast bubble of water and light and air, lost in the timeless flowing water and breeze.

He looked to his side along the boat. A long, rippling, green water snake, causing a quiet splashing of water, turned to him, its eyes cold, its tongue flickering up and down.

Ajay jolted.

In horror, he jumped up.

The sudden movement caused the boat to violently rock from side to side. Ajay screamed as it tipped, almost throwing them all into the sun-kissed water, where the long water snake was still arcing alongside them. Yasmin and Jai, unaware of the snake, cried out, putting their arms out to try and steady the boat, whilst Vinod used his saucepan to bail out water that had sloshed in from the other side.

For a moment, the world was shaking, out of focus. Then the boat steadied. Ajay clutching Kai and Saif, and all of them safe inside. The coppery-green snake, thwarted, moved its body viciously like a whip, and rippled away.

'What was that for?' said Saif, looking at Ajay.

'A snake,' spluttered Ajay.

Saif looked where Ajay was staring. 'You see a snake in the water beside you, and your instinct is not to stay safe on a rowing boat but to jump in?' he grumbled.

Ajay tried to think of a dignified answer . . .

. . . and was saved by a cry from Kai, who had been looking at his map and calculating the distance from one temple on the shore to another, to triangulate their position. He was now red-cheeked.

'Stop! We're here!'

They looked around at the jade-green water that rippled away from them in circles. Kai looked at his reflection in the wavy depths. 'I can't see anything,' he said, his eyes big and round.

Saif took out the fishing rod and hook that he had bought in Jaisalmer and attached a magnet to the end. 'We're in the right place – I'm sure of it. My calculations are never wrong. Move over,' he said, and energetically cast the line into the water. 'This won't take long!'

29

Two hours later: nothing.

The lake had become chock-a-block with boats full of families and tourists.

'I give up. You try,' Saif said in frustration, giving the rod to a startled Ajay. Chirping and squawking filled the air as a dove-grey cloud of birds flew up as one off the circular shrines in the water, beating their wings against the blue sky.

Ajay, still shaky from his encounter with the snake, flinched from the sound and sudden movement. He had been foolish to think Mr Jhoot was vanquished. What if Mr Jhoot sent more bodyguards – ones that even a crowd of yoga masters couldn't scare off?

'Are we definitely in the right spot?' said Kai, bending so far out of the rowing boat, that his nose almost touched the water.

'I think we should try over there!' said Yasmin, squinting a little into the distance and pointing to a patch of water that looked icy turquoise and was still in sight of two temples on the edge of the lake. 'The colour of the lake is different in that direction. It may be shallower.'

Jai rowed towards it. The metal magnetic hook Saif had wound on the end of the line caught something. Ajay tugged – and was almost pulled into the water.

'Help!' he cried. He was caught hold of by Jai, and Yasmin, and Saif, and Vinod, and Kai.

'*Heave!*'

They all heaved. The fishing rod bent, before pinging up, causing everyone to fall over and collapse on each other in a heap.

'I've got it!' shouted Ajay, catching the object that flew up like a cricket ball.

'You sure?' said Yasmin, scrunching her nose.

Ajay looked at the metal cylinder he was holding in his hand, full of sopping mud and green plants that squelched and stank. It looked like an old tin can. Kai pointedly held his nose. Disappointed, Ajay was about to toss it back in the water, when Vinod stopped him.

'Look underneath!'

Ajay saw that under the stinking mud, the cylinder was screwed together. When he cleared the muck, he could see that etched into the dark black-and-steel metal sides was the insignia of a dragon with amethyst eyes that looked right back at him. On the top was a dial with lots of letters around it.

'It's a tiny safe!' said Saif, his eyes wide with joy.

Ajay looked at it in awe. Until this moment, he hadn't been sure that the map truly would guide them to the Treasure.

'So, how do we open it?' said Ajay impatiently. The metal cylinder was cold to the touch and smelt of fish.

'I am an apprentice engineer,' said Saif grandly, taking the cylinder, which squelched under his touch. He sat down and twisted and turned it.

Eventually he looked up with a frown. 'No

good. This is some ancient technology made to defeat engineers. The only way to open the safe is to twist the lid so that we get the right word from the letters.'

Ajay felt his blood warm. Words were his life blood. They were alive to him. He took the can from Saif and inspected it. On the bottom of the can, his hand brushed some etched letters.

Yasmin sifted through her sketchpad, found a blank page, tore it from the book and, taking the can from Ajay, put the paper over the etched letters and began to rub the charcoal over it.

Words began to come through the paper, first elusively, like bark print, then, as Yasmin brushed the piece of charcoal to and fro, clearer and stronger: curved and beautiful.

'A riddle,' breathed Kai.

He was right! Yasmin held the charcoaled paper in front of her and slowly read out the words:

'What gives life—'

'The sun!' Ajay shouted joyfully.

'can sustain life—'

'Samosas,' said Saif definitively.

'and, like life, is fragile.'

Yasmin, Jai, Vinod, Kai, Ajay and Saif looked at each other, flummoxed.

'An egg,' said Vinod quietly.

The others looked at him, and then at each other. An egg?

An egg!

Ajay bit his lip. The six of them nodded. Saif turned the cylinder this way and that as they held their breath.

There was a sharp click.

The cylinder opened.

30

Conscious of the tourist boats that were drifting around them like iron filings pulled by a magnet, Ajay discreetly tipped the cylinder. Out of it came a small, square wooden box, intricately carved on all six sides. Ajay tried to prise open the lid, but couldn't.

'One riddle was too easy,' he grumbled.

'We could just smash it open,' suggested Jai with a shrug.

Kai grabbed the box from Ajay and threw a furious look at Jai. 'You're not smashing anything.'

Yasmin took the box and shook her head. 'Kai's right. Besides . . .'

Her fingers, long and delicate and graceful like a sitar player's, started shifting the tiny square pieces that sat on each side like a moving mosaic. Ajay watched, mesmerized. It was like watching one of those super-duper kids twisting a Rubik's cube so that all the colours were in the right place! Gradually, under Yasmin's hands the shapeless patterns began to take shape, until . . .

On each of the six sides of the cube was a picture of a different dragon. One with wings that arced into the sky, another with a long, winding neck with bristles, another with large eyes . . .

'They're fantastic,' said Jai. He touched the box with deep reverence, and gave Kai a look of apology.

Kai nodded, accepting the apology with aplomb.

Jai turned to Yasmin. 'How did you know that the dragons were there like that?'

Yasmin looked at the box and at each of the dragons, as if unable to take in that she had found them. 'I didn't,' she said hesitantly. 'I just felt that they were there all the time, underneath.'

'But we still don't know how to open the box,' pointed out Saif.

'That dragon looks like Kai,' said Jai thoughtfully. He quickly added diplomatically as Kai bristled, 'You know – courageous and fierce.'

Kai stopped bristling, and beamed.

Ajay looked at the dragon that had a snub nose and big eyes. It did look just like Kai – very stubborn.

Kai took the box and, looking at the dragon as if it were a reflection, rubbed the dragon's nose. The box opened.

They all gasped.

Inside was a small piece of vivid, moss-green cloth.

The others held their breath as Kai slowly unwrapped the fabric.

Inside the cloth, on a delicate silver chain with links that looked as if they were made of threaded light, was a single silver key.

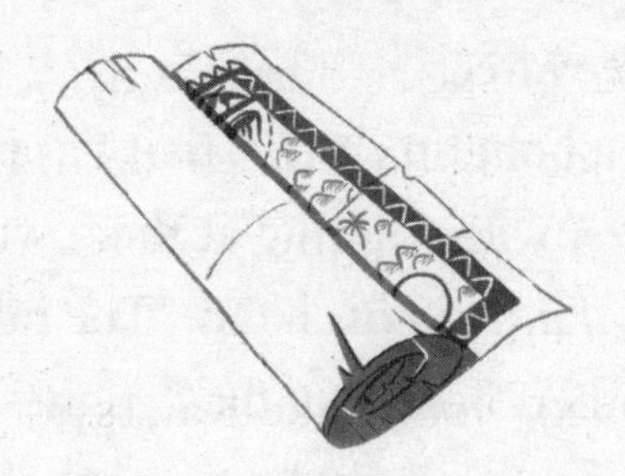

31

Ajay punched the air! They'd done it! They had found the first key on the path to unlocking the Treasure.

And what a key it was! It dangled from Kai's hand, spinning, winking blue and bright and silver in the light. It was whorled, and intricate and studded with a single tiny diamond that sparkled like a star.

Yasmin, Saif and Vinod clapped each other on the back. Jai tousled Kai's hair as Kai looked up at him in joy, his face bright with a wide smile!

'Hey – isn't that them?' A voice shattered their cheering.

Ajay twisted around, causing the boat to sway

again in the water.

A kid in a boat, in clothes that flapped like flags in the breeze, was pointing at them with a copy of *The Happy Paper* in his hand. 'The railway gang!'

On another boat, to their right, a snoozing family of four, on holiday probably, sat up. Copies of *The Happy Paper* fluttered off their faces, revealing expressions of contempt and revulsion. One started snapping photos of them with a phone.

'Thieves – stealing that nice Mr Jhoot's Treasure, no doubt!'

Vinod's face tightened, strained. He put a saucepan into the water, ready to start rowing. 'We need to get out of here.'

Yasmin's head jerked up, and Ajay saw her usual self-possession snap as she faced the family. Her emerald eyes went pitch dark, like storm clouds filled with lightning. 'We're not stealing anything.' Her voice choked with fury. Her words echoed brokenly across the lake.

There was a cry from behind Ajay. He whipped around. The kid had thrown a pebble, grazing Jai's cheek and leaving a small streak of red. Jai, wincing in pain, put his hand to his cheek to stem the blood.

The kid throwing stones grinned. The pebbles plopped in the water around them like tiny explosions.

One landed near Kai, causing lake water to splash him in the eye. His face – which just a moment ago had been jubilant – rippled in a mix of shock, and pain, and confusion. He looked up at Ajay and said something, but the words came out as a whimper.

Ajay bit back the bile in his throat.

Kai. How to shield him?

He put his hand on Kai's shoulder.

'It's OK,' said Ajay. He didn't recognize his own voice.

Kai looked up at him with trust in his wide eyes.

Ajay took a deep breath. Keeping his hand on Kai's shoulder, he turned to the others, his voice ringing with command. 'We get out of here. Now!'

For a moment, they sat still – and Ajay saw Yasmin, shuddering with resentment, desperate to fight back, even knowing that she would lose. He held his breath and her gaze, which was both troubled and furious. At last she nodded. Jai took the oar, Vinod took his saucepan, Yasmin (after a moment's more hesitation) and Saif took a stick each, and all four started to row as one.

The younger children in the family started booing and, encouraged by the two adults, started throwing crumpled sheets of *The Happy Paper* at them. The kid in the other boat continued to throw stones and whistled tauntingly at them.

As their boat rowed away, back into the gentleness of the lake and forwards towards the shore, Kai stepped closer to the shelter of Ajay's arm, clutching the key in his hand. He sniffed back tears.

Kai was crying.

How dare anyone make Kai cry?

Ajay's self-control unravelled. He shook uncontrollably and delved into his memory for something – anything – to help him regain control.

And through the waves of darkness and nausea rolling over him, his mind hooked on a memory.

The day he had celebrated his sixth birthday.

A passenger calling him stupid – and spitting on him.

Sitting in the corner of the platform and rocking himself, wordlessly.

Niresh, the Mumbai railway station attendant, bringing out a basin of warm water and a thick hot chocolate, flavoured with enough red chilli and cardamom to make Ajay's eyes tear up with water that had felt like a relief.

What was it that Niresh had said?

Through the rage burning inside him, Ajay's mind twisted and turned, searching for the memory.

When dignity, home, and even hope, are stolen – find courage.

And then, in his soft voice, Niresh had recited a poem. At the time, Ajay had barely caught the words. Now fragments and flashes came to Ajay through the darkness, swirling like hot sparks.

Under the bludgeonings of chance

My head is bloody, but unbowed.

Ajay lifted his head.

Rage had burnt its way through him. And in its

wake was knowledge and resolve.

He was the editor of *The Mumbai Sun*.

Ajay turned to Kai with a fierce protectiveness. 'It's OK, Kai. I'll take care of you.'

Kai sniffed, nodded, and huddled closer in.

Ajay gently put his arm around Kai's shoulders as they stood together and watched the water, lit in a wash of gold and orange by the setting sun, flow across the side of the boat, slapping softly against its sides.

Ajay held his mother's pen in his hand and his mouth settled in a stubborn line.

The past helped to navigate the future.

He remembered what he had said to Jai about Muhammad Ali, and drew a deep breath of inspiration and promise.

The Happy Paper had just picked a fight with the wrong opponent.

32

The next evening, Ajay was standing on the outcrop of rock, rising from the ground, that was marked on the map and looking down at the crumbling ruins of an abandoned village. A light, swirling wind, carrying with it the smell of herbs and decay, had picked up and was now blowing fistfuls of sharp dust in their faces. Flickering shadows at the bottom of the empty buildings almost looked alive.

'I'm not sure about this,' murmured Yasmin against the wind, holding her arm to protect her face from the stinging particles.

'It's definitely the right place,' said Saif staunchly, unconsciously flicking Ash's coin, looking at the village below them. Deep, rich, amber-dark sunlight flooded through the alleyways and lit the stones that made up the broken buildings. 'According to the map, this is where we find the second key.'

A mix of adventure and excitement and dread bubbled up inside Ajay. There were only three days left until the Auction where, if he found the Treasure before them, Mr Jhoot would sell it. And then it would be bought by a billionaire – perhaps taken out of India – and disappear for ever!

'Let's hurry,' he said.

They started to move, slipping and sliding through the rocks to get to the half-eaten walls of the abandoned village. Ajay crouched and stumbled, scratched by thorns and dog-eared plants. Stones and pebbles clattered and washed against each other as the others tried to find their way through.

'I don't like it,' said Vinod, as they helped each other up and stood at the front of the walls of buildings that once, perhaps, had been full of life, but were now filled with an eerie silence, punctuated by that sharp, whistling wind.

Kai was reading from his book, *The Traveller's Companion to Thar* – the one the map had been hidden in – his eyes round like plates with excitement. 'This is Kuldhara – the ghost village.'

Ghosts! Ajay rubbed his hands with glee. First a quest, and now ghosts. The story for *The Mumbai Sun* kept getting better and better.

'Perhaps we shouldn't be here,' Yasmin whispered softly.

Ajay looked at her in surprise. When had Yasmin ever backed away from anything? Even now he could feel her resentment that he had asked her to back away from the fight at the lake, smouldering like ashes in every word she spoke to him.

'Nonsense!' said Saif boldly. 'I'm an apprentice engineer. We deal in facts and physics!' He looked at Yasmin and added kindly, 'Ghosts are not real.'

Yasmin shot him a look to freeze the dead.

The group split up, on the hunt for anything that might help them find the Treasure. Ajay and Kai found themselves stumbling completely alone through the village, where the sunlight ran like liquid gold. An eagle swooped across the sky, wheeling back sharply as it spied its prey moving in the distance. The last of the sunlight caught in the bird's bronze wings as it dived downwards, its claws flashing.

'Let's look at the map,' said Ajay uncertainly.

Kai took it out, biting his lip in a way that Ajay often caught himself doing. Ajay saw the care with which he unrolled it, making sure that the parchment did not tear. Together they carefully laid it on a flat stone and pored over it.

Again, Ajay was left speechless by how intricate the map was. He could see the fine line produced by the fire that had led them to the cross in the desert – and just before that, the outcrop, and next to it, the cross that marked the spot they were in now – the ghost village. But he couldn't see anything that would help them work out *where* in the village the next clue to the Treasure was.

A group of small birds settled on to the high wall next to them, which had a crescent etched on one of the stones, and watched them with beady interest.

Kai picked up the map, turning it. 'Ajay . . .'

Kai was pointing to an oily smudge on the map.

As Ajay looked, he realized that the mark was not a smudge at all, but a drawn, shaded circle.

One of the birds gave a shrill, haunting cry.

A sudden gust of wind blew dirt into Ajay's eyes, and he rubbed them with both his fists before opening them and looking upwards.

A dust storm!

All thoughts of the map were whisked out of his head. The dust storm was swirling around him like a fog of gold. It blinded him, choked him, strangled him.

It was turning into a funnel, and starting to glow with an inner light.

Its mouth was becoming wider and wider.

Ajay lost sight of Kai.

He was all alone.

And inside the mouth of the glittering dust, Ajay could see darkness. And inside the darkness – a small figure outlined in golden dust particles.

'Mother!' he shouted.

33

It was the image of his mother.

Outlined in dust, she looked older than he remembered. Her sari clung tightly around her wraith-like form. Her eyes were alive with longing – as they had been the day she had abandoned him.

Ajay cried out.

He ran forwards, into the swirling darkness, reaching towards her.

Her image shifted, and Ajay saw next to her another vision . . .

A young Ajay, trotting proudly beside his mother on the railway platform. Enough rusty coins slipping out of the little cloth bag to feed them for four meals.

A half-broken umbrella lying in their path, its broken metal spokes splayed like spider's legs.

Ajay's knees crumbled.

He tried to cry out a warning, but choked.

His younger self tripping – falling – causing the coins to cascade into the cracks of the platform.

His mother looking at him, her face filled with anger.

Was that when she decided to leave?

He reached out.

And, like a sandcastle in water, her image dissolved at his touch.

He screamed, ran, trying to chase the specks as they scattered away from him.

'Ajay!'

He heard Kai's voice next to him; felt Kai's small hand grip his.

Not again. He couldn't bear it to happen again.

'Ajay!'

Kai's voice broke through the nightmare. 'It's a ghost, Ajay! A trap! Come back!'

Ajay turned to Kai. Kai was looking at him in stark fear. Ajay felt the tug of the vortex – the tug of his mother spiralling away.

'Come back!'

Ajay turned back to Kai, torn between his past and his present.

With a cry, he grasped Kai's hand.

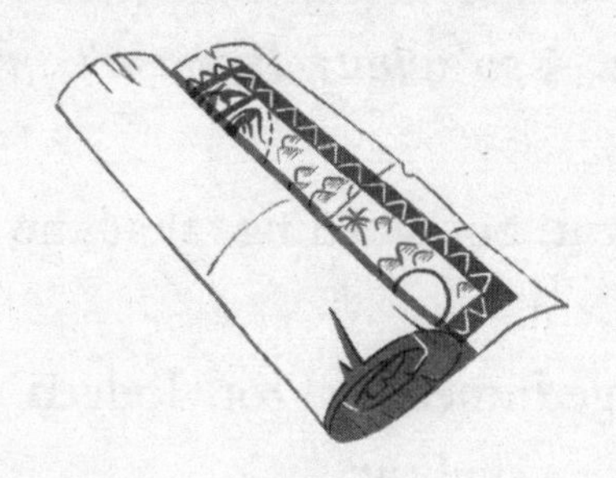

34

It was like being pulled from dark and swirling quicksand.

Ajay gasped, spluttered.

In his mind's eye, he could see the form of his mother calling him – voicelessly – through the storm.

The dust pulled away a little, and Ajay saw that if he had run forward, following the scattering images of his mother, he would have fallen on a pile of jagged, shiny rocks.

As he looked at them, he remembered again what he had buried deep inside for so long – tripping and falling, and her sudden, vivid anger . . .

I tripped – so what? It wasn't my fault that she left.

A thought so startling that he could not breathe.

The jagged metal razor lodged inside him shifted ever so slightly.

He held tightly to Kai's hand and looked away from the rocks.

He owed Kai his life.

Ajay turned to face him, but Kai's lip was trembling. He stared over Ajay's shoulder. 'Look!'

Ajay looked. Kai was pointing towards the outer edge of the glowing dust storm that was circling around them both.

It parted and, outlined in gold, Ajay could see his four friends facing their own terrors made real – Jai crouched, Yasmin standing, Vinod huddled, and Saif with his fists in his eyes to hold back his tears. All unaware of him, and each other.

Jai – strong, powerful Jai! – was putting his hands up in front of his face, against a glittering dust shadow looming over him. Ajay and Kai ran towards him.

Jai looked at them, his eyes stricken.

Kai stood between the shadow and Jai, his hands on his hips, a tiny figure against the looming darkness.

Ajay held Jai tightly. 'We're with you now.'

Jai slowly stood up and gazed at the shadow.

'You defeated this shadow once. You can do it again,' Ajay shouted, above the keening, haunting wind.

The past had no right to haunt them.

At Ajay's words Jai stared down his past. Slowly the shadow began to shrink

. . . and shrink

. . . and shrink

until it was smaller than Kai.

It was a tiny ball of whirling darkness, the size of a golf ball.

Jai stepped forwards and, with tears streaming from his eyes, hit it with his bat.

It spun into the crackling purple vortex – and vanished!

Jai stared in its direction, looking shocked for a moment that it had actually gone. That he had vanquished – for the time being, at least – his past!

Kai and Ajay linked arms around Jai's shoulders,

and the three pressed their heads together. Then, as one, they rushed towards Yasmin.

Yasmin's face was strained. Her arms were pushing away thick, hard lines of compressed sand that were enclosing her – trapping her.

Jai ran forwards, using his strength to back her up, his shoulder muscles flexing, sweat dripping from his forehead.

Kai and Ajay went on either side, crouching like wrestlers against the bars of sand.

'You can't imprison me,' Yasmin said steadily.

As the four of them battled on every front, the bars shook.

Confidence shone out of Yasmin and exploded in a dazzle of light.

The bars flipped, spun out in all directions.

Without any resistance, Ajay, Kai and Jai staggered before collapsing on their knees on the ground. Exhausted, breathing hard, Ajay's bones weak.

Yasmin looked at them and her eyes sparkled with green fire. She pulled them up.

They ran to Vinod.

He was no longer huddled. Even without them

he had managed to get to his feet, his fists clenched, his wiry form strong against the wind.

His eyes were fierce and filled with lightning. 'I don't need your permission.'

'He's already a cook,' Ajay informed the vortex, his voice echoing down the funnel. Then added for good measure, 'Not just any cook. The very best cook in Mumbai!'

The winds died down, with a sound suspiciously like a stomach grumbling plaintively.

Vinod gave a grim smile.

'Saif!' shouted Jai, and they all ran to him.

Ajay looked at him. Saif looked so sad! What was haunting him? A nightmare about failing as an apprentice engineer?

'Saif, what's wrong?' Yasmin whispered at his side. 'What did you see?'

Saif looked at her with great gulping sobs.

'A world . . .'

The others looked at each other with consternation and shuddered. What sort of ghost world could have upset Saif so deeply?

Saif continued to wail noisily. 'A world without . . .'

The others waited in terror as he wiped away his tears.

'A world without any samosas!'

Saif hiccuped.

The others collapsed over him, giving him a big hug.

35

Ajay sat together with the others in the middle of the village, exhausted, but feeling strangely light and happy.

It was close to midnight. They were huddled around a crackling fire that Vinod had made, drinking cups of soothing jasmine tea to keep warm. Saif was reading from his magic book to comfort himself. 'Train your body to eliminate any movement that will tell the audience what your next move is,' he murmured, and then, turning the page continued, 'Your attitude as a magician is essential to ensuring your success. Be relaxed and your movements will be invisible to others.' He looked at his hand and flexed his fingers thoughtfully.

Ajay looked around. The village still felt full of ghosts – not the kind that made Ajay's skin prickle like sand ants, but rather ones that were more human. Ghosts that, like them, had lived and loved; suffered and grieved.

The constellations glimmered in the sky like webs of platinum. And hanging like a giant orb amongst them all was the moon.

'I've never seen the sky like this,' said Yasmin softly, illuminated by the bright firelight, tugging a cloak Vinod had given her around her shoulders. She waved to astronaut Anita as Ajay had done.

It was true – the moon was throwing light like silver paint over them all.

And suddenly, Ajay understood the clue in the map!

He had no time to explain. Taking one of the burning sticks from the fire, he held it like a living torch and started running north.

Sweat poured down Ajay's face as he ran, conscious of the others dousing the fire and running behind him. Finally he got back to the place where he and Kai had been standing before the vortex had appeared. He stood in front of the wall, looking upwards to where the small birds had been seated and where one of the stones was marked with a sign of a crescent.

'Could you stop this obsession with walls, houses and dragons?' Saif puffed after him.

'Shush,' whispered Yasmin in awe. 'Look!'

The moonlight, like molten metal, fell on to the wall. As they watched, breathless with astonishment, the light, strong and intense, slid up. In a silvery blaze, it hit the stone with the sign of a crescent.

'The map!' shouted Kai, jubilant. 'The smudge that's a circle! It's the full moon.'

And in that moment, the single ray split, filling the wall, pulsing light through the cracks in the stone.

Ajay ran forwards, shielding his eyes, as the light shot and sparkled like silver fire.

He called to Kai and lifted him on to his shoulders, shifting so that Kai's weight and jabby feet didn't hurt as much as they had in Mr Jhoot's office.

As he teetered and balanced, he heard Kai pull out the stone with the mark of a crescent – a sharp, scraping sound. Kai leapt off Ajay's shoulders and landed with a thud. In his hands was a small wooden box marked with the sigil of a smiling dragon with outspread wings and talons.

Jai, Yasmin, Saif, Vinod and Ajay linked arms around each other's shoulders as Kai rubbed the dragon's nose to open the box.

Inside, wrapped in folded layers of dark cloth, was a second silver key.

Kai took it out and, delicately, it glimmered and twirled on its chain.

Capturing Kai within their circle, they spun around so fast that Kai's legs lifted off the ground.

36

The next day, Ajay and the others met the childhood friend of Kai's Grandmother – Daksh. Reading the note she had written for him, Daksh had agreed to drive them as far as he could across the Thar desert.

'What is this?' said Saif, his face livid green as they rushed up a particularly large sand dune in Daksh's dune buggy. 'I am an apprentice engineer – not an action hero.'

Ajay wanted to answer, but his bones were rattling up and down as the buggy – a vehicle like a small van that could ride through the sand – went up and up and up the sand dune, towards the sun's scorching hot light. Jai and Yasmin were yelling in exhilaration at the tops of their voices, whilst Vinod and Saif had grabbed tightly on to each other. Kai's head was half out of the buggy window, looking as if he were on the best roller-coaster in the world!

With a jolt, the buggy dived, cruising down the dune's slippery slide, in a rush of sinking sand.

And before Ajay's stomach could catch up with him, they were rushing up another sand dune.

With the two keys in their possession, they were on their way to the location of the red cross on the map.

Ajay felt his stomach lurch.

When they reached the top of the final sand dune, his face was as green as Saif's.

'We're here,' said Daksh, as they all clambered out and stood looking down on the curves and hollows of the desert glowing under the hot, blue sky.

Ajay swallowed, mopping his face, feeling the blistering heat gathering around him. Looking at the desert, it was as if he were a tiny piece of coloured glass spinning in a kaleidoscope.

How vast the world was.

Yasmin gently put her hand on his shoulder, as if anchoring him to the ground. He shook his head to clear it.

Daksh, silent and tall, belonged to the desert. 'Tell your Grandmother that I said hello,' he said suddenly to Kai, his topaz-coloured eyes full of light. 'We used to dig for fossils together – no one knew more about the desert than she did.'

'She doesn't remember as much any more,' said Kai hesitantly.

'Your Grandmother lived the life of legends.' Daksh looked out at the waves of dunes stretching out in front of them like a sandy sea. 'That can't be taken away from her.'

Kai bowed his head, and Ajay felt his chest constricting.

Saif, flicking Ash's coin across his knuckles with unconscious ease, was staring at the map, then blinking as he looked out at the curving, sinuous sand dunes.

'The dune buggy can go no further, so the rest of your journey to the oasis marked on the map will need to be on a camel caravan. The oasis is long gone. But the camel riders will be able to show you where it once lay. These might help you to get to their camp,' said Daksh with a smile on his lean, weathered face, untying ropes that tethered something flat to the top of the dune buggy.

Ajay and his friends looked at each other.

Surfboards?

Dune-boards!

The next moment, Ajay was watching the others careening down the final sand dune. Jai and Yasmin standing on the boards, elegantly swishing and sliding, as they raced each other, their boards carving swerving lines in the sand. Vinod was sitting on his, going carefully, using his saucepan occasionally to help him out when the surfboard stalled. Saif had fished around in his pockets, found bits of wire and a battery pack, and created a makeshift motor to add to the end of his board. It roared to life! The surfboard flew into the air, with Saif on top of it. Then it crashed on to the sand, which flew sharply, stinging from all directions. The board whizzed forwards, outracing Jai and Yasmin, until Saif was a speck in the distance.

Ajay and Kai were the only ones left. Ajay bit

his lip. He had not dared admit to the others that he was scared. He liked heights! He liked speed!

He did not like the possibility of falling.

If only Kai had been scared too. Then Ajay could be as brave as a lion for him (it was always easier to be brave for other people!). But Kai had explained merrily that he had done this before – and looked expectantly at Ajay to get on, so that he could follow.

Ajay stood gingerly on the dune-board like Jai and Yasmin had done . . . and wished almost immediately that he hadn't. The board wobbled and teetered. The sand dune was very high up and the scene in front of him swam and shimmered in the boiling light.

'Not like that!' Kai called out, shaking his head. 'Like this!'

Ajay turned his head and saw Kai, looking annoyingly comfortable, standing on the dune-board next to his, pushing his spectacles back in place.

'You have to find your balance,' Kai said, adding complacently, 'It's easy when you know how.'

Easy to say when you were six (or thereabouts) and close to the ground! Not when you were Ajay and could trip and break your bones.

'I know – I'll help,' said Kai, getting off his dune-board and coming around to Ajay.

Ajay's eyes widened. 'I don't need—'

'I don't mind,' Kai said, shoving him and the board off the top of the dune.

'—your help!' Ajay screamed, turning to the front.

The board tore down the rippling sand, and wind and grains blasted towards him. Ajay's stomach toppled, and his feet whisked out from under him, causing him to slam with a thud on to the front of his body, grappling the sides of the board with both hands. His eyes closed. All he could feel was motion, and the lurching of the board against his ribs. His stomach was in his mouth. The board slithered and gathered speed.

'Hold on tight!' Kai's voice came from a distance. For a moment, Ajay thought he was dreaming, but then from the corner of his eye saw Kai calmly surfing a dune-board parallel to him.

Ajay opened his mouth to snap at him, but got a large mouthful of dry, gritty sand instead.

He choked, spat it out.

'Try to get up on the board,' said Kai next to him, now balancing on the dune-board with one leg.

Slowly, Ajay raised himself up on the board. It started

to turn, and for a moment spun so that Ajay was sitting upwards.

'The other way!' Kai said helpfully next to him, whilst doing a headstand on his.

Ajay gritted his teeth and, against the tug of gravity, tried to get up again.

The dune-board spun again, so that he was at least now facing the right way!

With his muscles tugging and his limbs aching, Ajay trembled and slowly, leaning forward, got to his feet.

For a second, he toppled, righted himself again, and then was standing.

Or rather surfing!

Ajay gasped. He had never felt joy like this! He was cresting the waves of sand dunes. He was an eagle! He was flying! Suddenly he was part of the blazing blue sky, the rich red-gold sand, the cold, sharp wind. And then, as he rollercoastered downwards, the past and future didn't exist. Just that speeding, freeing moment!

'Are you pleased I taught you?' said Kai smugly, keeping pace on his board, curving and arcing next to him.

Kai had shoved him, not taught him!

But Ajay was too happy to give Kai a sharp response.

He could see in the distance the small camp of tents Daksh had told them to aim for. He headed straight for them, swerving neither left nor right, speeding up, feeling weightless, rushing onwards as the camp got bigger and bigger . . .

Until—

Ajay went flying forwards, off the board, landing face down.

Splat!

Ajay wiggled his toes and hands to check that they were in working order. Then he cautiously lifted his head. It was plastered with sand which, when he blinked, fell in little rivulets from his eyelashes.

In front of him Kai, Vinod, Jai, Yasmin and Saif were crouched down, turning their heads to his eye level, peering worriedly at him.

'You OK, Ajay?' Saif asked.

Behind them were the long, droopy faces of camels, and the proud ones of the camel riders. The smell of campfires and the warmth of camel breath filled Ajay's nose. They had made the camp!

Ajay beamed at his friends, the camels and the camel riders.

The Mumbai Sun would soon have its exclusive. The Treasure was almost in their grasp.

Then, the smile still on his face, exhausted and exhilarated, Ajay's head dropped back into the sand.

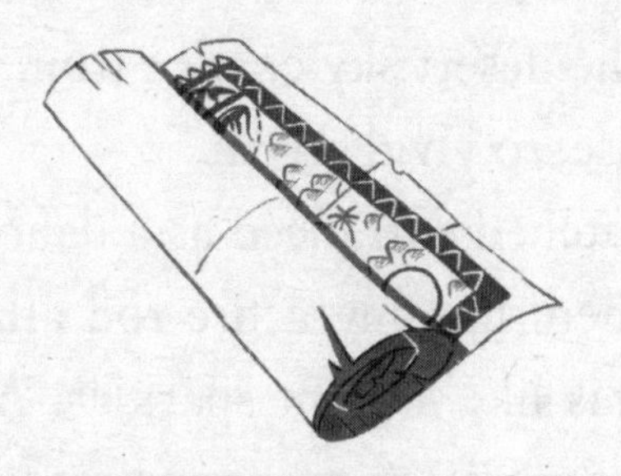

37

The fire flared, shooting out a gush of starry embers. Warmed by the flames, and the toasted roti he was eating beside it that cracked between his teeth, Ajay felt his blood tingle and spark.

They were in a desert camp on the way to the oasis. Ajay found it strange to think that the oasis itself no longer existed, and that the only reminder that it ever had was the single tracing marked on the map.

On hearing their story, and the name of Kai's Grandmother, the proud camel riders had let them join their evening campfire. The team sat around, the flames flowing over their features, as they watched the desert sky change from blazing blue, to turquoise, to vivid green.

Ajay watched entranced as a dancer whirled in front of them holding a fire rod aflame on both ends. It was like a giant sparkler! As the dancer spun, the flames left wavering traces of warmth and gold and red behind, like writing in the darkening sky. They all clapped in time to the thrum of the music and for a moment, Ajay felt the intoxicating stir of glinting stars, flame and sand.

He inhaled deeply – smoky air, spiced with the scent of burning embers, pepper and sandalwood.

'Ajay – look at Ash's coin,' said Saif, snapping shut the magic book he had bought in Jodhpur. He held the coin with a falcon on it out in his palm by the light of the crackling gold fire, then swiped his hand across it. It vanished.

'Where's it gone?' said Ajay, looking around the shifting sands that glittered darkly around them. Tonight he could believe in magic.

'It's on your shoulder!' Kai whispered in awe, his eyes wide behind his owl-like glasses.

Ajay stood up and turned his head, trying to look at it, but Saif clasped his shoulder.

'Look in your pocket,' Saif informed him.

Ajay dug in, and found it. Saif gave a wink and a bow.

They all clapped.

'Thank you,' said Saif, blushing modestly. 'It's taken me a long time to master that.'

'How did you do it?'

Saif waved them away. 'An apprentice magician can never tell his secrets.' Then, too excited to stop talking, he started explaining. 'Really, it's about misdirection. No one can focus on two things at once. They just imagine they do. So, I make you look here.' He demonstrated again. 'And do something over there,' he continued, catching the coin from the air. 'It's wonderful,' Saif added, and there was genuine wonder in his voice.

Ajay was still blinking. In some ways, magic was the opposite of a newspaper. People read newspapers to learn the truth; they watched magic to allow themselves to joyfully be lied to!

Ajay frowned. That was the problem with *The Happy Paper*. It pretended that there was no difference between truth and lies. And then used the confusion to stir up hate. Ajay shook his head.

He had to fight it.

But how could he, and *The Mumbai Sun*, win?

Yasmin was flicking through her sketchbook beside him. Ajay gasped – and worry about *The Happy Paper* took flight. A flick-book! Yasmin had drawn a copy of the mogul princess with a falcon (from Mr Jhoot's private collection) in soft pencil lines. As the pages flicked in the half-light of the fire, the falcon soared through the enchanted tissue of the paper as if in flight.

And then, when that drawing finished, there was another one that began to play! A moving drawing of the six of them hugging each other and jumping up and down. The best she had ever done – it wasn't just that they seemed alive; it was as if they contained in their lines and shading her very blood. Yasmin noticed him looking at the drawings, and in the wild firelight her face looked older – she had poise, and confidence in her eyes.

For a moment, he did not recognize her.

'Why did you draw us?' Ajay said, smothering down the strange sense of loss. 'You see us every day.'

Yasmin smiled at him, and the smile made his

blood sing. 'So that if I'm ever sad again, I'll remember what it was like being happy.'

Sad? A sudden hollowness opened in Ajay's heart. She hadn't ever confided in him when she had felt sad.

When had she been sad?

'Does it make a difference?' Jai interrupted softly, turning to them. 'When you are unhappy? Remembering times when you weren't?'

Yasmin looked at Jai and nodded vigorously. 'Doesn't it you?'

He hesitated, and Ajay's chest hurt as he watched her hand lightly touch Jai's in comfort.

Kai, who had gone with Vinod to get snacks, popped his head between them and pushed his way to sit down between Yasmin and Ajay with a plate-ful of crunchy fried golden kachori with spiky mint chutney. Glad of a distraction, Ajay made room for him next to the curve of his arm. Wiping a smear of chutney from around his mouth, Kai gave one kachori to Ajay, then gobbled the rest. He wiped the oil off his fingers fastidiously and brought out his suitcase, taking out the map and staring at it by the light of the fire.

'It's so near,' he whispered, as if unable to believe they were really there.

Ajay looked up, wanting to change the mood. He turned to the others, brightly. 'What's the Treasure going to be?'

'A dragon!' Kai shouted at once, and, firmly pushing back the soreness in his heart, Ajay cuffed Kai playfully around the head.

Corrupt billionaires and hateful newspapers could be dealt with, but a fire-breathing dragon would be a step too far – even for the mighty *Mumbai Sun*!

'Magical gold coins,' said Saif, tossing the coin Ash had given him up into the air. It disappeared mid-flight, only for Saif to then find it behind Kai's ear – to Kai's bouncing delight. 'They'll turn me into Saif the Sorcerer and Master Engineer! People will come from far and wide. I'll astonish them with magic and science!'

He threw the coin up again . . .

Yasmin snatched it from mid-air, her eyes dancing. 'An emerald flying carpet. I'll fly across the world on it, drawing everything. And people . . .' she added dreamily, 'people I'll never meet will see my drawings and, for a moment, even if they are lost, feel protected against the cold. They'll feel safe and not alone.' She held the coin for a fraction longer, then tossed it to Vinod . . .

Who caught it and turned it over slowly in his hand, a strange yearning in his black eyes. 'A box of magical spices.' He looked up at them all. 'To make the food I cook so good that people lick their lips and—'

'But they already do that,' said Saif, shaking his head, confused. 'You should ask for something better . . .' His eyes went wide with the answer. He stretched out his arms. 'Like a record-breaking-sized samosa!'

Vinod grinned, and spun the coin towards Jai.

Jai picked it up and stared across the sand dunes, blood-red in the low setting sun. He stirred the sand with a stick. 'A gold orb, that will make me the G.O.A.T,' he murmured at last. 'So I'm never afraid of him again. What about you?' he asked Ajay hurriedly, before anyone could ask any questions about who 'him' was. Jai handed the coin over, his gold eyes dark. Ajay took it from him, keeping his thoughts from appearing in his eyes.

Jai's safe now.

Ajay held the coin in front of him like a ring.

The team turned to Ajay expectantly, excitement shining out of their eyes.

'What else?' Ajay said cheerfully. 'A magical printing press that will make me editor of the most famous newspaper in the world!'

The others laughed loudly. When the laughter died down, they patted each other on the back, fizzing with anticipation for the day to come, finding places on the warm, yielding sand around the fire to spread out the blankets the riders had given them, and settle down to sleep.

Ajay watched his friends, and struggled. How could he tell them the truth? He wanted fame and fortune! But everything else he really wanted – had ever wanted – was within this circle.

Ajay took out his mother's pen and twirled it slowly between his finger and thumb so that it spun around, flashing gold and black.

Almost everything.

38

The next morning, at dawn, Saif was standing looking up at camels.

In return, they looked down at him sleepily, their long-lashed eyes hooded, and gentle expressions on their mouths. One with knobbly knees, who clearly had taken a shine to Saif, bent its neck and nipped his hair, and he glowered back at it.

'The riders will lend us five camels to take us to the place where an oasis once existed. We need to choose them,' he informed Ajay, before waving him off. 'Give me some time. The secret is looking at their teeth.'

Ajay was flummoxed, but left Saif to it, with the others all packing up and getting final supplies ready. He climbed up the nearest sand dune. And then, alone for a moment, he took a deep breath.

Dawn in the desert was beautiful. The crystal light edged into fragile gold, deepening into the colour of grain. In front of him were endless dunes. No shadows, just a white brightness that hurt his eyes.

He turned and saw one of the youngest riders (about twelve, the same age as them!), who Ajay had heard called Ali, trudge up the dune. Ali had loose brown clothes, round features, wide eyes and a shock of unruly hair. As he walked, each foot went plunging into the glittering sand, which scattered as he trod. He was carrying extra weight!

'A falcon!' Ajay cried. He had never seen one up so close before. Its fierce face was amber, and its feathers a sparkling mix of copper, emerald, and bronze.

Ali nodded proudly. Adjusting his stance, so that the falcon was balanced as it climbed up his arm, he waved at Ajay to come nearer. 'I'm training it! Want to try?'

Ajay bubbled with excitement as Ali gave him a

heavy emerald falconer's glove to wear and, with the falcon giving a screech in protest, transferred the bird to Ajay's arm.

Ajay held it in shock. The falcon was huge!

It turned its head at face height and stared unblinking at him. Its eyes were jet black, it had a small ring around its leg, and its beak and talons were sharp enough to pinion and claw Ajay with. He saw his reflection in its eyes, and stood, measure for measure, mesmerized. He shivered with anticipation. He had never been close to anything like it. Sometimes, at the station in Mumbai, when it was cold and wet and he was sitting looking at the spluttering light of a lamp, Ajay longed for a dog by his side. But everyone knew that railway kids didn't get close to animals. Railway kids could barely survive on the food they had; they didn't have any to spare.

He felt a sudden gust of wind graze the side of his face, causing the falcon's feathers to bristle.

'Lift your arm!' cried Ali, a gust of excitement rippling across his features. 'Quick!'

Ajay obeyed, raising his arm up against the sky. The weight of the falcon suddenly released as it soared upwards, its gorgeous feathers shimmering rust and copper in the morning sun. With its wings spread, it flew further up and up into the air. Ajay felt his heart take flight too, and, for a moment, they were joined as one. It was as if he were the falcon. Through its unblinking eyes, Ajay saw the burning gold sand dunes, felt the rush of cold air racing against his feathers, the twisting roar of hunger in his stomach, and the smell of fresh meat in his heart.

And then, forged together with the falcon, high above the landscape, he glimpsed the path he and his friends had to pick through the towering sand dunes to a sparkling, fluted marble pillar that marked the Treasure of Thar.

Along the path, in his mind's eye, a monstrous sand snake, coiled and glittering, was heading in the same direction.

'Watch!' Ali breathed next to him.

At his words, Ajay was suddenly separated from the falcon and back inside himself, his heart hammering.

Was I imagining it, or did it really happen?

The falcon spotted something, circled, and

dived down sharply, like an arrow, hurtling towards its prey.

The snake?

They couldn't see it, but Ajay imagined the battle between the falcon and the monstrous serpent. The serpent rearing its head, the falcon flashing down, its talons sharp. The serpent twisting round, its poisoned tongue flickering out, and hissing. The falcon veering up to escape, only just in time.

They saw the falcon arc back, its talons empty. A little less power and strength in its wing beats.

It flew towards them, but now, small as a tiny needle glinting in the sky, it seemed a hatchling, cowed and beaten. It looked so young and afraid as it circled above them.

Ali tugged Ajay's arm. 'Can you do this?' He let out a series of three low whistles. Ajay licked his lips, practised a few times (there were times when Ali had to stuff his fingers in his ears) then nodded.

Fingers in his mouth, Ajay blew three loud whistles.

For a moment – nothing.

Then, the falcon stopped mid-flight. Had it heard?

They watched as it dived down, slowly at first, then more confidently, to Ajay's outstretched hand . . .

It landed. Ajay puffed with the full impact of it and almost toppled over. It weighed a ton!

'Watch out,' Ali said, with a grin, pushing him back up to steady him, and Ajay stood with the falcon on his arm, looking into its dark eyes set within its amber face. The falcon preened its feathers and shook out its wings, bending its head. Ajay didn't dare comfort such a wild thing, but he made some low noises in his throat to show that he understood – that it wasn't cowardice to back away from the snake at that moment, but survival.

Another time, the falcon would win.

He and Ali put their arms around each other's shoulders, in a shared moment of joy.

'She's magnificent!' Ajay said, as the falcon flew over to Ali. He felt a sudden sense of loss.

Ali nodded, caressing the feathers on its back. 'You know her call now – whistle when you see her, and she will come!'

'Ajay! Hurry up!' He heard Saif's call echoing from far below the sand dune. 'The camels are ready!'

Ajay squared his shoulders, and grinned goodbye to Ali.

It was time to find the Treasure!

He looked the falcon in the eyes once more, and his heart thudded in his chest.

39

The camel ride was sweltering, long and very bumpy! Heat radiated from the ground, like an oven, and sweat flowed down Ajay's face as he rode forwards, perched on the camel's hump. From time to time he looked down, feeling dizzy. The sand was scratching his eyes! And the red-hot dunes wobbled under the camel's steady, silent tread.

Hours later, and with many miles crossed, it was time for the camel riders to take their leave. They whispered to Saif and disappeared silently into the wind. Ali turned back to Ajay and gave a final wave, his falcon spreading its wings so that they glinted in the light.

Saif stopped, consulted Kai's map, and got down from his camel. Ajay's camel turned its head, snorting warm air at him in amusement.

'We're here,' Saif said definitively. 'According to the riders, it's where the oasis used to be.'

The camel dipped its neck and knelt, and Ajay slid down its back with a whoosh on to the sand. The others did the same.

'Are you sure?' said Jai, shielding his eyes as he looked into the sun's glare, his camel kicking beside him like an Arabian horse.

Ajay bit his lip. The sand dunes stretched out endlessly before him, blood-red, moving sinuously in the wind. The shimmering heat weighed down on all sides, making him feel like he was being broiled alive. Feverish and disconnected, he tried to clear the sweat from his eyes. His head hurt.

He was the editor of *The Mumbai Sun*. What was he doing miles away from home in the middle of a terrifying desert?

'Have some of this,' said Vinod worriedly, passing him a flask of wild mint tea given by the riders. Ajay drank thirstily, feeling his mind clear with each freshening drop. He looked around. Nothing. And then, suddenly in the distance, he saw what he – as the falcon – had seen. A pillar of stone, scoured by the wind into a strange and fantastical shape, fluting upwards, veined with sparkling stones that threw out a rainbow of light. Hope and energy sprang up in his body.

'Over there!' shouted Ajay.

They had crossed miles to find the Treasure. They weren't going to be defeated now!

He saw Kai's face shine with hope, and grinned.

His camel knelt and Ajay clambered his way back up, then led the others forward towards the marble pillar. But now the wind, the hot breath of the desert itself, picked up, and without the camel riders to guide them, the camels became fractious and agitated. The sand stirred, swirled and sifted around him, turning the air into a hazy yellow and red. Ajay gasped. Everything tasted of sand, and he started to cough.

'Ajay!' Jai threw back a rope to him. Ajay caught it, tied it, and threw it back to the others. They were connected, and their camel train drew strength. They inched forwards. The sand filled Ajay's nostrils, his ears, and stung his eyes – covering him with grit, blurring his senses.

Pain filled his chest.

He kept moving forwards. And then, just when he was shaking with terror that he had taken a wrong turning in the blinding heat of the sand, he was at the foot of the marble pillar.

For a moment, seeing the white plinth in front of him, Ajay could not trust his eyes. He rubbed them raw, freeing them of sand. It was still there!

Buffeted by the winds, he looked up and up and up at the pillar. It rose in front of him like a mirage, twisted and strange and magnificent, towering far above them like a shimmering castle of crystal.

Ajay and the others slid down the backs of their camels. Jai tethered the camels safely together.

'Ajay, look!' Kai whispered beside him.

At the base of the pillar was etched the sign of a dragon. Its two wings were spread out and at the tip of each wing were the talons, and at the tips of the talons were two keyholes!

'The keys!' Ajay cried.

Yasmin brought out one, Vinod the other. The keys dangled on their chains, sparkling like splinters of stars. Yasmin gave hers to Ajay. He watched Kai take the other from Vinod. Kai was covered in red sand, but his eyes were bright – and suddenly Ajay remembered, like one of Yasmin's moving images, all the moments with Kai layered on top of each other like traced tissue paper.

Present and past and future felt like they were happening at the same time.

Ajay's heart ached. Once they found the Treasure, Kai would leave and he might never see him again.

Kai smiled trustingly at him, and Ajay swallowed.

I lost Mother and survived. I can survive losing Kai too.

And deep inside him came a sudden cry.

How many people can I lose before I can't stand it any more?

Kai, unaware of Ajay's thoughts, looked at him questioningly.

Ajay pushed back his emotions and forced a smile. They were on the brink of finding Kai's Treasure! The legendary Treasure of Thar – kept secret for centuries.

'Kai – are you ready?'

Kai, standing at the other keyhole, nodded.

'One . . .'

They both pushed the keys into the lock. They clicked into place.

'Two . . .'

Together they turned the keys.

Ajay could hear a metal mechanism swinging into place; the unlocking like dominoes of machinery.

'And . . . three.'

Ajay held his breath, waiting for the pillar to open and reveal the Treasure inside!

Nothing.

Disappointment hit him like a wall.

Was it all a hoax?

Ajay saw Kai's face fall, and Yasmin, Jai and Vinod hold each other against the battering swirl of sand, and Saif drop to his haunches, failure scrawled over his face.

Ajay opened his mouth, to say something – anything to ease the hurt of his friends.

But before he could . . .

. . . the desert trembled.

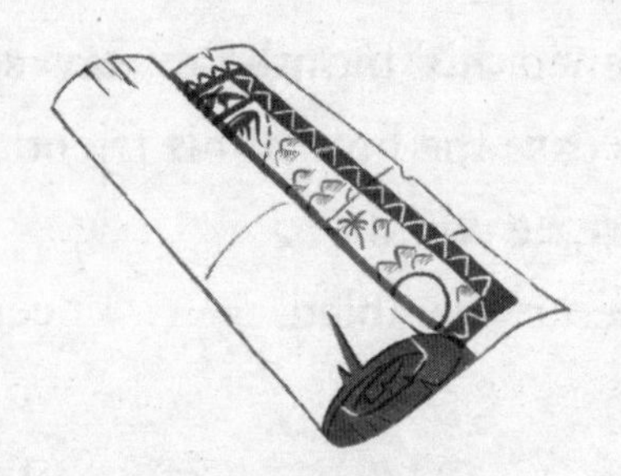

40

'What's happening?' shouted Jai. He reached out to the others, creating a shelter with his arms. They huddled in each other's warmth, against the hot lash of wind and bite of dust. The camels bit through their tethers and galloped away from them.

A crater was opening up under their feet. Sand was falling in a soft rain from the edge then pouring in, in fine, sifting waves that drummed against their ears.

'Ajay!' Kai sobbed.

Ajay tightened his grip on Kai, as the others tightened their grip on him.

The crater was heaving open. Jutting out of the

fissure was what looked like the top of the roof of a sandstone fortress.

Ajay stepped closer to the edge of the crater and looked down. He fell to his knees, his mouth open in awe. He had seen such wonders – but nothing like this. The domed roof of the building buried below reminded him of the pictures he had seen of the Jain temples in Ranakpur, but instead of being carved with intricate religious figures, this was carved with flying fire-breathing dragons!

'Let's go!' Kai cried, jumping ahead despite the heat, sliding on a lick of sand to get down to the arched gateway of the ornate fortress being revealed within the crater's depths.

Ajay and the others raced to chase him down to the entrance and followed Kai into the giant arch.

Ajay blinked as he walked through the dark archway into a small cool room. He had thought it would be dark inside, but instead the fortress that towered around them glowed rippling green from hung copper lamps.

'Ghost-lights!' Saif whimpered.

The strange light flickered over the intricate carvings inside, creating shadows and movement as the sand dragons seemed to fly in the lamplight. Kai was racing through, into another patterned doorway.

'Wait!' Ajay cried.

Too late. Kai was through.

And then, from the next room, came his shattering scream.

41

Ajay leapt through the doorway and was immediately plunged into the darkness of a second room, twice as big as the first.

'Kai!'

A low sob of fear.

Ajay turned to his right and his eyes adjusted. He saw Kai plastered to the wall to his side.

Beyond the thin ledge in front of him . . .

a sheer, sandy drop into nothing.

'It's OK, Kai,' said Ajay, moving crab-like along the ledge, a river of sweat running hot down his back, making his shirt stick to his skin.

Kai ignored him and, shaking, pointed to the wall opposite.

Ajay looked up and saw why. Over the chasm, on the opposite wall, was a green-gold, hammered-metal image of a dragon with glowing red eyes that illuminated the darkness. It looked so real – its eyes fierce; its mouth open; its mighty wings stretched out against the wall.

Jai, Yasmin, Vinod and Saif burst in through the door next to them.

'Stop!' Ajay cried. They heard – just in time – stones skittering at their feet, dropping down into the gaping emptiness of the fissure.

A splitting crack.

Ajay looked up as the metal dragon's mouth opened.

A wave of heat streamed through the room.

A stone shot out, fizzing hot and trailing gold sparks, and hurtled towards him.

'Watch out!' he yelled, and ducked, shielding Kai as the stone crashed into the wall where his head had been. The wall cracked under the stone shards that hammered into it. Pieces of the wall fell, cutting into Ajay's back. Ajay's ears rang like an iron bell, as smoke hissed out of the hole.

He knelt, putting his hand on Kai's shoulder.

'We're going to get through this, Kai!'

Kai looked up at him, frozen in fear, and Ajay saw a graze on his cheek from a lone spark from the stone.

'I'm going to try and get across,' shouted Jai. And before Ajay could stop him, Jai took one end of the rope, ran and took a flying leap. He landed – only just – winded, on the ledge below them on the other side of the gap. Ajay could see his shoulders heaving with the effort and his exhausted dark figure bend and tie the end of the rope he was carrying to a stone. It went taut, slanting downwards as, on Ajay's side, Vinod tied the other end to a jutting piece of rock. Now they needed to use it to cross the chasm.

Ajay gulped.

More fireballs shot from the dragon, increasing in number, heat and soot and fiery flames coming straight at them. It was like a horrible game of dodgeball.

'I'll go first,' said Vinod lightly.

Before anyone could argue, he had gripped hold of the rope with both hands and swung below it.

It held!

For a moment, it looked easy. Then Vinod cried out in pain. His arms stretched, and looked as if they were being pulled out of their sockets by his own body weight. Ajay could see the veins in his arm muscles spasm.

'Vinod!'

Vinod's mouth was held in a tight line, his teeth gritted, sweat on his brow. He was clearly in too much pain to answer. Dangling below the rope, he started to move, fist over fist, across the chasm, making it to the other side as Jai hauled him to safety. Saif and Yasmin went next. Saif first, curled up like a koala on the rope, murmuring: 'I am an apprentice engineer. I have muscles of steel'; Yasmin's face was grim, her knuckles white.

Another fireball shot out, missing Saif.

Yasmin swung her body left, out of the way, but her skirt whipped the edge of the fiery stone. The skirt caught fire, trailing purple and gold incandescent flames.

'Yasmin,' Ajay screamed.

Like a burning firework, she toppled on to the other side, with Jai and Vinod smothering the flames before they could hurt her.

Ajay's stomach convulsed. Saif collapsed in a heap on the other side.

Two fireballs, like twin missile rockets, shot out of the dragon's mouth.

'Jai, watch out!' Ajay cried.

Jai held up his bat, and – with the strength of ten tigers – hit one. It slammed into the other, so that both flew across the room. There was an explosion and a swirl of blue heat, as both incinerated with a bang.

'It's our turn now, Kai,' Ajay coaxed and reached for him. Flying detritus was exploding all around them.

Kai, with the bravery of ten lion cubs, gripped Ajay's hand with his tiny one!

Ajay held on as Kai stood from his crouched position and the two of them stepped to the brink of the ledge, facing the others opposite.

'I'm going to get you on the rope. Don't look down.'

Kai looked down and shook.

'It's just like the dune!' Ajay said hurriedly. 'And I'm just here. If you fall, I'll catch you. But you can do this, Kai!'

Ajay, with his heart in his mouth, helped Kai on to the rope, using his extra shirt to help tether him securely like a grip wire.

'I'm going to let go now,' Ajay said, speaking softly.

And then Ajay let go. Kai, holding on to the shirt, slowly slid along the rope, until he was hanging from the middle of it, dangling above the yawning chasm. The shirt was holding!

Ajay hurriedly swung on to the rope. He looked down once at the empty void underneath and broke out into a cold sweat.

One fist in front of the other.

The rope swung gently. Ajay heard the image of the dragon, hissing, about to throw out another fireball.

He ignored it, concentrated and got to Kai, who was snuffling quietly.

'It's OK to be scared,' Ajay whispered as he reached him.

Kai slowly opened his eyes.

On the rope, Ajay felt the strain on his arms. His hands, slick with sweat, were slippery; his grip was loosening. He needed Kai to hurry, but he didn't say anything. Just waited, hanging there above the sheer fall.

He saw Kai gather his strength. He saw a look of determination cross Kai's face.

And then Ajay saw Kai swing to gather momentum.

One. Two. Three!

Kai started to slide!

Faster and faster, the slide gathered speed in a rush.

Ajay was left behind on the rope. 'Wait for me!' he cried as he hurried after him.

'Yippee!' Kai shouted in delight, as he gripped

on to the shirt and hurtled down the wire, straight into the arms of the others!

Ajay crashed in after him. Vinod helped him up.

Kai was already standing, being patted on the back by the others, wreathed in smiles.

He turned to Ajay with his old confident brazenness.

'Can we do it again?'

Ajay stared at him. *Do it again?*

Did Kai not recognize that Ajay had risked life and limb to get him across? Ajay opened his mouth to give Kai a piece of his mind but was saved from replying by Jai calling them over and pointing: 'The door's underneath the dragon's mouth. We need to hurry.'

Saif had cut the rope and coiled up the rest on to his shoulder. He nodded to Ajay.

At Ajay's signal, Saif, Jai, Vinod, Kai and Yasmin stood in a line. Then they ran forward, through the door below the dragon's mouth, into the next chamber.

42

They had to be close to the Treasure now!

As Ajay ran out of the Dragon's Hall to the room in front of him, it went dark. His eyes adjusted. The walls of the second room were made of sand that gleamed like wet gold. In the centre of the room was a circular sandpit.

Unable to look away, he walked towards it.

Kai was lecturing the others behind him: 'A second challenge! The fireballs were all about courage – I passed,' he added smugly. 'So this one must be about skill.'

Ajay was barely listening. A large circle had been drawn in the sandpit, and within it was a single, cloudy, crystal marble, the size of a golf ball. Outside the line, sitting on a stone pedestal, were three smaller marbles that glinted in the light of the flaming torches that surrounded the pit. Ajay felt his blood rush inside him, his cheeks turn warm and his hands itch to play. Every railway kid loved a game of marbles – and Ajay had never seen marbles like these before!

Reverently, he picked up the three small spheres of glass and swirled them in his hand, so that they clashed and clinked together like ice. Inside the centre of each glass orb were the smallest carvings of silvery-blue falcons looking ready to take flight.

Three chances to push the crystal from the centre of the circle.

This would be easy!

A burst of flame shot up in front of him, blinding him for a moment.

'Ajay!' Yasmin's voice was a warning.

The flame rippled around the drawn circumference of the circle. Ajay jumped back, only just avoiding getting scorched. A ring of fire. He watched the flames in alarm, his confidence evaporating. The only way of hitting the crystal would be to flick the marbles with his fingers like a catapult so that they flew over it.

Saif looked at the flames, then at Ajay. 'Well? Hurry up. Play.' At Ajay's hesitation, he said in a tone of infinite superiority, 'It's just a matter of angles and force and mass.'

'And skill!' Kai repeated under his breath.

Ajay slowly knelt in front of the circle. The flames rippled and danced in front of him, creating waves of heat. Beyond them, the crystal glowed. Ajay measured out the distance: from where he was sitting, all the way to the centre of the circle. His knees hurting, he pressed his thumb into the ground, and using his middle finger angled one of the marbles.

Then he flicked it. It launched into the air and rolled on the compacted sand towards the crystal . . .

. . . and missed it by a centimetre.

Ajay closed his eyes, and his body trembled. A sense of failure washed over him.

There was the sound of rumbling over his shoulder. He opened his eyes, turned, and he and the others yelled in terror as part of the ground collapsed with a crash into a yawning hole.

For a moment, he stared as a cloud of sand rose into the air.

A third of the ground had vanished into an abyss. No one could survive that drop!

Vinod put his arm on Ajay's shoulder in wordless support.

'Two marbles left!' Saif squeaked. He frowned at Ajay. 'You must calculate your angles!'

Hastily, Ajay positioned himself again. Two more chances.

His throat dry, he got the marble ready, and flung it with his middle finger . . .

. . . and knew he had made a mistake with his aim. The marble was flying too far to the right.

'Stop!' Ajay whispered.

The marble landed to the right of the crystal. Ajay's heart dropped painfully.

There was a low groan from the ground behind him, and as he twisted around another third of the floor crumbled into a void, scattering sand everywhere. Yasmin, further back than the others, hurriedly ran, leaping forwards – only just getting to safety.

Ajay shuddered. The others, clutching each other, stared back at him, wide-eyed. Would they be next?

The pressure grew around Ajay's head, like a pan of water reaching boiling point.

Needle-like pain lanced through him.

Ajay stared, feeling sick in his stomach. The last marble. His last chance.

He focused on the crystal, his stomach churning. If he missed again, it would all be over. Sweat beaded on his forehead. He wiped it away. He readied again, but his hand was shaking.

'You're forcing it,' commented Jai softly. 'Clear your mind. Forget the crystal. Just enjoy playing the game.'

'Enjoy playing?' Ajay turned to him and let loose his frustration. 'How exactly, when the ground is collapsing?'

Jai shrugged helplessly. 'It's what people always tell me.'

Ajay held the marble in his hand, feeling its heavy weight and how cool it was in the heat-soaked room. Thoughts of the cloudy crystal, the Treasure, and the ground collapsing invaded his mind. He shook his head and tried to focus on the memories sparkling inside him: the shot of joy when he had found his first midnight-blue marble in the street gutter with his mother; Niresh, the station attendant, buying him a pack of small green glass marbles and patiently teaching him how to flick them; playing with ruby-red marbles with Vinod by the station.

Enjoy the game.

Ajay stilled his mind and concentrated on his breath.

With everything he had, he flicked the third and last marble.

It arced in the air, catching the light . . . then fell, hitting the crystal so it rolled out of the flaming circle . . . unscathed.

'Bull's-eye!' he whispered.

He had won!

The others sprang at him and hugged him, holding tight as a square of ceiling opened above them, creating a whirlwind. The marbles flew into the air in a spinning tornado and vanished upwards.

'What did I say?' Saif said, stepping back, and

nodding as if he, not Ajay, were responsible for the win. 'Angles.'

Ajay's smile became wider. They were free to continue to the Treasure!

And then the floor tipped and sloped.

Ajay and his friends slid down, plunged into thick, smoky darkness.

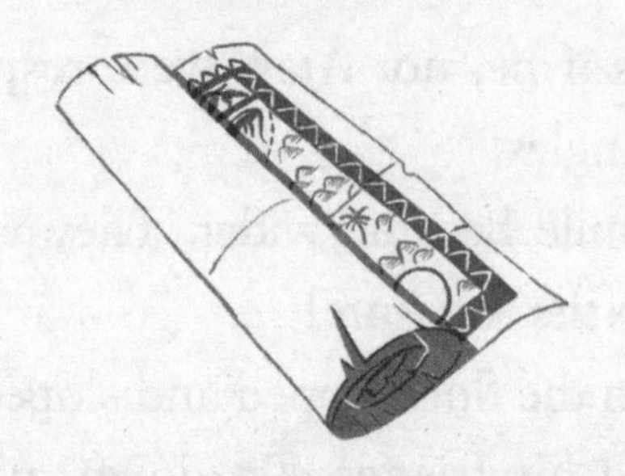

43

'The final challenge,' Kai said confidently, jumping up from where he had fallen on the floor of what must be the room below. 'In legends, they always come in threes.'

Ajay picked himself up painfully, dusting the sand that came off him in clouds. He felt a moment's pang for the beautiful, deadly marbles. Then he shook his head and concentrated. They had to find the Treasure of Thar before Mr Jhoot, and soon – for the story for *The Mumbai Sun* and for Kai!

The room they were in now was even spookier than the others.

'Where are we?' said Vinod.

'The heart of the fortress, perhaps?' whispered Yasmin.

Ajay agreed. It was a room of sand walls that glittered with dragon images, gold and red in the light of flames. And in the centre was a small lake of crystal-blue water, with curls of hot mist breaking over the surface.

He moved towards it, keeping a tight grip on Kai who looked excited enough to just jump headlong in. Ajay remembered how thirsty he had been crossing the sand dunes, and his throat convulsed. So much water, here, in the heart of the desert, made him feel dizzy!

At the edge of the lake, he looked in. The mist cleared, until the surface shone as sharp and silvery as a mirror. Ajay could see his reflection, and that of Jai, Vinod, Yasmin, Kai and Saif.

The image spasmed, changed, and it was no longer of the five of them.

The reflection that now looked back at him was of him – but not of who he was now. It was of him as an adult!

Ajay stilled, unable to look away. He saw himself as he had always wished to be – bold and fearless; unshakeable confidence in his eyes; sitting in a chair at the head of a table at *The Mumbai Sun* holding his mother's pen; vivid excitement playing across his features and a bar of sunshine from a window making a gold crown of light on his hair. Around him, he could hear the soft cries from the others.

'A master engineer!' Saif exclaimed joyfully.

Did they all see their dream versions of themselves too?

He saw a small path emerge, leading to the centre of the lake, formed of slippery hexagonal sand stones.

'This way!' he called to the others.

They picked their way across the stones: Saif admiring his reflection in the lake; Vinod looking thoughtful; Yasmin's eyes bright with dreams; Jai taking long, relaxed, powerful strides; Kai running as quickly as he could in front of them.

In the centre of the lake, there was a hexagonal shaped stone, large enough for all of them to stand on one side each – with a circle carved in the centre. As they stood facing inwards, the circle cracked open and a pillar twisted out.

They gasped.

On the pillar was the most beautiful crown Ajay had ever seen! It was made of filigree silver work and tipped with pulsing blood-red rubies and ice-white diamonds that scattered rainbows.

'Look at it!' whispered Vinod.

Ajay trembled.

All the joy and confidence he had felt only moments ago vanished.

He felt feverish. It felt as if his heart had been cracked open, and inside all there was, was a deep hot desire for the crown. It would make him rich – he would never need to think about money again! If he took the crown, he would feel the one thing he had never felt in his life after his mother had abandoned him – safe. Salty wet tears, from nowhere, sprang up in his eyes. What would it be like to not shudder for a moment every time you woke up? He would do anything to feel safe and protected again.

'It's so beautiful,' cried out Yasmin, her hand going up to touch the spokes encrusted with rubies.

My crown!

'Don't go near it,' Ajay hissed, his throat clogged up.

And suddenly, looking around, through the curling watery mist, he saw Jai, with his wolfish grin, a thug who could take the crown by force; Yasmin, with her distant, cold smile, a thief who would steal it and disappear without a look or word; Saif, his cunning rival, creating machinery that would make him a titan of power; Kai. How small and pathetic was Kai? Ajay almost snarled. A heavy burden with jabbing feet, trapping Ajay into looking after him and draining him of money and time. As for Vinod . . .

Ajay stopped.

Vinod.

Just his name was like a cool thought.

Vinod – his oldest friend. The gentlest of them all.

He looked at him, and shook. Vinod had fallen to his knees, his hands in front of him, as if single-handedly fighting back a horde of invisible ghosts. He looked back at Ajay and his eyes were alight with pain.

'Fight back!' he whispered. 'Remember who you are.'

Remember.

Ajay blinked, shaking himself free from the coils of the poison. He saw his friends – their faces contorted by envy, anger, ambition and greed. Their eyes opened wide, reflecting the internal battle waging inside them.

Ajay ran to Vinod, helped him up. Then, as loudly as he could, he shouted, 'Don't let it win!'

At his words, one by one, the others snapped back to the friends Ajay recognized – Jai, Yasmin and Kai – their faces still harrowed by guilt and horror at who they had become.

But Saif was still looking at the crown, his eyes aflame, his hands moving towards it.

'Saif!' Ajay cried.

Saif turned, his face in shadow.

For a moment, the air between them stilled. Ajay felt his mind swirl. If Saif became his enemy . . .

'Saif!' Ajay cried again, and his voice broke on the name.

Saif blinked. 'Ajay?' he said softly, his eyes wide.

There was a bright flash of light, like the flare of magnesium.

The crown, that had almost destroyed them, disappeared.

For a moment, Ajay felt his chest constrict – if he had only grasped the crown he might have felt safe for ever.

He shook his head.

'Good riddance!' he muttered.

In the crown's place was a huge, fossilized egg. Ajay felt a weight lift from his chest.

An egg?

'What's this?' said Jai, mystified.

Kai's eyes were full of dreams. 'Can't you see? It wasn't the crown at all. *This* is the Treasure of Thar.'

44

'The great Treasure of Thar is an egg?' Saif, fully recovered, looked affronted. 'We have battled snakes and camels' (Saif's camel had nibbled away at Saif's hairline, and he had yet to forgive it) 'and crossed miles of desert, all for an egg?'

'Not just any egg,' whispered Kai. 'A Dragon's Egg!'

Jai bit his lip. His eyes met Ajay's over Kai's head and he shrugged. Kai caught the look. 'You don't believe me!' he cried.

Before Jai could explain or apologize, the hexagon slab started to shake underneath their feet. They all looked at each other.

'Sandquake!' squeaked Saif.

The still water of the lake became choppy, sloshing over the edges of the slab and across the path of hexagonal stones, its water ice-cold.

Ajay's legs slipped from underneath him and he swung out wildly with his hands to steady himself. Around them, the lamps swung, creating moving pools of shadows. The wall beside them started to crumble, letting forth a torrent of sand that started to blast in hot fissures at them.

'Run!' shouted Ajay, as hot sand started to pour in through the perforations in the walls.

Kai scooped up the heavy Egg, almost toppling with its weight. Jai picked Kai up, despite Kai's indignant protests, and raced ahead, taking two steps to everyone else's one. Vinod and Yasmin flew after them, Yasmin's hair streaming behind her like a banner. Ajay and Saif brought up the rear. They ran along the stone path, the slabs shooting up into jets of hot air behind them like machine gun fire. The ceiling half-collapsed, causing a flash of blue sky. The sand flooded in.

'Ajay, help!' shouted Saif. Ajay half-turned and saw Saif behind him, caught in a moving tongue of sand. Ajay's heart stopped; his stomach churned.

Without thinking, Ajay dived in.

The sand covered him, suffocated him, buried him under its grainy dark weight. Everything went black. He pushed his way up, and up, coughing as his head broke through the sand's surface, and he could breathe again. Using every scrap of energy and life he had, he waded across. He pulled Saif up, spluttering.

'Ajay! Catch!' Jai shouted from above the crater, where the ceiling had once been, throwing one end of the rope down towards him. It fell, slapped into the sand . . . and sank. Ajay waded towards it, catching it with one hand, holding Saif in the other. The rope slithered rapidly through his fist, burning and scraping his skin raw. Just at the last moment, Ajay managed to tighten his grip. The rope scratched his hand into bloody streams.

'Now!' he shouted to Jai.

He heard Jai shout to the others: 'Go!'

Ajay felt a tug on the rope. He screamed in agony as it cut into his gashes. Slowly, as the sand filled the hole, lifting them towards the gap in the ceiling, Ajay and Saif were dragged, twisting on the rope, upwards.

Just as the crater was about to be plugged with sand, they reached the surface. With a mighty heave, Jai put his arms around Ajay's chest, whilst Vinod and Yasmin did the same for Saif.

Slowly, bit by bit, they dragged them out, away from the whirling sand trying to suck them back in.

Ajay leant, then toppled, against Jai.

Am I alive?

He collapsed in a heap on the surface. Exhausted.

His breath rasped, his lungs were shredded, his body heaved.

Ajay turned his head to the light of the desert sun. It shone on him, bright and liquid and warm where just a second ago there had only been suffocating sandy darkness. He squinted, forced his eyes open and saw the others. Jai was on his back, breathing deeply, his hand flung across his face; Yasmin was curled up against the sand, her hair matted, her eyelids closed; Kai was sitting hunched up, clutching the Egg. The camels had returned and were bent protectively over Vinod and Saif (Saif's camel was tenderly nibbling his hair).

'Are you all OK?' Ajay whispered.

One by one, the realization that they had survived dawned on their faces. Saif and Vinod got up from where they had been kneeling on the ground. Ajay felt his terror subside. His bones relaxed into jelly. He was filled with a slow, seeping sense of relief.

And then, looking at the

Egg, he suddenly felt a blaze of happiness warm him!

'We've escaped?' breathed Yasmin.

'The Treasure!' shouted Kai.

Their faces filled with awe and disbelief. They had done it!

Ajay and Kai pulled each other up and laughed, and hugged each other, each of them holding the huge, blackened, fossilized Egg in turn, marvelling at it. It might be just a giant egg – but it was *their* giant Egg.

The Egg that had started a quest, brought them together – and *might* belong to a dragon!

Kai had got his Treasure, and Ajay had his story for *The Mumbai Sun*!

Just wait until he got it printed. The whole of India would sit up and take notice!

'I'm so glad that you survived,' a voice said behind them, in rich tones that echoed the sound of dripping coffee.

Ajay whirled around.

It was Mr Jhoot.

And with him, a jeep that was spilling out a unit of grim-faced bodyguards.

45

'Go away!' shouted Kai. He looked up at Mr Jhoot, furious and scared. 'This is my Treasure – you're not getting it!'

Mr Jhoot smiled, emanating charm, his brown eyes full of warmth. He waved back the bodyguards and stepped forward, kneeling slightly so that he was more at their height. His voice was gentle. 'Ajay. Kai. You shouldn't have run away from my party,' he said softly. 'I was trying to help you. Why didn't you stay? We could have found the Treasure of Thar together. We could have been allies and avoided all this unpleasantness.'

Ajay looked at him in confusion.

'You can still trust me. Look – I want to do

what's fair.' His eyes were friendly. 'I have a deal for you – the dinosaur's Egg for a hundred rupees. You can't say better than that!'

A dinosaur's Egg? Ajay and Yasmin looked at each other. Ajay felt his heart thrum. Of course! Not a dragon's egg, but a dinosaur's! The Egg was thousands of years old! And suddenly he remembered the various names of dinosaurs that had thrilled him to his fingertips – Tyrannosaurus Rex, Diplodocus, Brontosaurus. Something in him remembered the time before people – when India was full of roaming beasts. He breathed out loud.

'No,' said Kai. 'It's not for sale.'

Ajay saw Mr Jhoot's smile waver.

'That is a shame,' Mr Jhoot said. He clicked his fingers, and the bodyguards marched over. In one swift movement, they took out solid metal bars and slowly – deliberately – covered them with sharp steel barbed wire that glinted in the sun's light. Jai, his eyes narrowing, took out his bat. Vinod, wrath unleashed in his eyes, took out his saucepan.

Ajay pushed Kai, holding tightly on to the Egg that they had saved, behind him.

'You're threatening us?' said Ajay, furious.

Mr Jhoot looked at him. 'I am not doing anything,' he said, his voice sounding gratingly reasonable. 'This is your choice, remember?'

'Some choice,' murmured Jai, keeping an eye on the bars covered with barbed wire.

Ajay looked at Mr Jhoot and felt his skin crawl. Who went from charm, to blackmail, to violence without stopping for breath?

A python – a predator that preys on those who trust him.

Ajay shivered – this was his fault; once he had put Kai and the map in Mr Jhoot's sights, there was no escape. Mr Jhoot lived only to exploit others – coil around them, then squeeze until they shattered.

'You are so rich. How can you possibly want more?' whispered Yasmin.

Mr Jhoot's eyes grew big, shining with innocence. 'You took *my* map,' he whined.

For a moment, Ajay questioned reality. Then he felt like laughing out loud. Did Mr Jhoot honestly think that he was justified? Entitled to keep hurting them?

The urge to laugh stopped. That was what made Mr Jhoot so dangerous, Ajay realized. There was no guilt, no apology, no sense of the difference between truth and lies, or right and wrong – no sense that he had *enough* without needing to destroy others to get more.

Mr Jhoot would never stop hurting them because he liked the power of squeezing people until they bled.

They had to get away.

Ajay warily watched the bodyguards surround them.

And if they couldn't do that – they had no choice but to fight. Not just for the Egg but for the right to be free from Mr Jhoot's control.

The others caught his signal, and crouched. Saif had fashioned a catapult with the rope. Ten bodyguards to the six of them.

We can do it. Jai, Yasmin, Vinod, Saif, me and Kai. We can beat him.

Mr Jhoot looked as if he had made the same calculation in his head. He smiled.

'Ajay, do you know what every good negotiator needs?'

Ajay felt his blood freeze.

'A trump card. It is how I succeed in business. You see, most people look for *what* makes people vulnerable. I have a different approach – one that always wins. I always find out not what, but *who*, the other side is willing to die for.'

Mr Jhoot gave a signal.

Two bodyguards came down from behind the sand dune. And pulled along with them, bound and gagged, her eyes fiercely bright, was Kai's Grandmother.

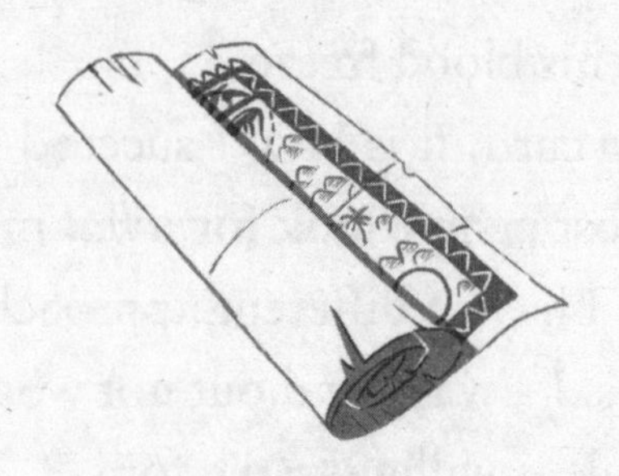

46

'Grandmother!' Kai cried out. He looked up at Mr Jhoot – panic in his eyes. 'Let her go!'

Ajay felt fear like he never had before. His tongue became thick. He wanted to double over.

What would I have done if Mr Jhoot had my mother?

Anything.

Mr Jhoot smiled at Kai. 'Daksh was willing to tell me the secrets of the map to ensure your Grandmother's safety. Now it's your turn. Give me the dinosaur's Egg.'

Kai ran up to him with the Egg. 'Take it.'

Mr Jhoot took the fossilized Egg carefully in his hands. He was shaking. His eyes glistened. 'The

Legendary Treasure of Thar.' He let his hands touch its surface.

He looked up at Kai sadly. 'This is your fault, you know. If you hadn't been so difficult,' he continued softly to Kai, 'your Grandmother would be safe now. This is on you.'

Ajay felt sick.

He plays mind games. He finds people's weakness – then burrows, poisons and twists.

Ajay whispered, 'You won't get away with this.'

'With what? This is your choice. You are making the right decision and returning what's mine. I'm not threatening you.'

Ajay stared at him. Was he joking? He literally had a blade at Kai's Grandmother's throat.

'Let her go,' Kai whispered again, his arms outstretched towards her.

Mr Jhoot's face was amused as he looked at them.

Ajay felt his heart turn cold.

Mr Jhoot turned to the bodyguards, and instead of releasing Kai's Grandmother, their grip on her tightened. A desert truck came into view, and more units of slick and lethal bodyguards flooded out, surrounding them.

'Let her go?' Mr Jhoot lightly held the Egg as if it were a toy he was already bored of, and smiled. 'Now, why would I do that?'

47

Mr Jhoot's guards took Ajay and the others to Jaisalmer Fort, tied them up and left them alone in a room where the last of the afternoon light sifted in through a grimy window.

'Well, this is a good pickle we've got ourselves into,' Saif complained from the chair he had been tied to. He had been grumbling steadily now for the last two hours. 'The Auction is tomorrow – where the Egg will be sold to an international buyer, never to be seen in India again. All of us are tied up – hungry' (Saif sounded particularly aggrieved at the last point) 'until we agree to sign a false confession. *The Happy Paper* that has made everyone hate us is the most successful paper in India and . . . have I forgotten anything?'

Yasmin lifted her head. 'The camels.'

'Ah, yes – the camels.' Saif's face fell, filled with worry. 'Cut loose into the desert where Nibbles will probably starve.' He sniffed, and a big, fat, glistening tear rolled down his face.

Jai looked exhausted, sweat dripping from his face, his eyes barely opening. He had been quiet for hours, just straining his muscles, hopelessly.

There was the sound of a crash to his side. Kai, trying millimetre by millimetre to scrape his chair towards his Grandmother, had fallen sideways with a thud, causing him to cry out in pain as his shoulder jabbed into the ground. His glasses scattered across the floor.

Kai's Grandmother, still gagged, looked at him, wild with anguish.

'Kai!' shouted Ajay, flushed and hot, leaning with all his might towards him. It was no good! The rope on his wrists held, and just dug deeper.

'I'm OK,' Kai said bravely.

'We've got to get out of here,' said Vinod, carefully angling his chair nearer Kai's Grandmother in reassurance.

Ajay needed to clear his head and plan. 'Saif – the book you bought in Jodhpur! Did you learn anything to help in that?'

Saif sniffed. 'I only got halfway through the chapter on "Escape like Houdini!". There was a lot going on. You know – sandstorms, being chased, collapsing ceilings, and Nibbles ate my—'

'You're our only hope,' said Vinod gently. 'You have to try.'

For a moment, Saif looked panicked at the responsibility. Then he squared his shoulders, closed his eyes and frowned. 'Let me think.' He began to recall things from his memory: 'Keep calm . . . a master magician is always prepared . . . don't freeze; be more polar bear . . . your muscles are at their most alert when most relaxed . . . expand your awareness . . . find an opening . . .' His eyes opened. 'It's no good,' he said frustratedly, in abject defeat. 'I can't do it! I don't know how.'

'Try again,' Yasmin said softly. 'No one knows everything when they start.'

Vinod nodded.

Saif steeled himself. Closed his eyes and

whispered, 'Houdini said his brain was the key that set him free.'

Ajay held his breath.

Saif opened his eyes and looked at the others, nodding to himself, suddenly confident. 'I too have a very big brain.'

Everyone went quiet. Saif flexed his arms, slowly working one loose. He stopped, breathing heavily, his eyes watering with effort.

There was silence.

Then the sound of popping.

Ropes slid to the ground.

Saif opened his eyes – in joyful triumph.

48

The first thing Saif did was to help Kai up, give him back his glasses, and remove the gag from Kai's Grandmother's mouth. Then he and Kai freed the others.

They stood together, Kai's Grandmother still seated, nursing her wrists, vivid intelligence and love in her face, as she kept an eye on Kai, who was bursting with energy, ready to go at Mr Jhoot.

'What now?' said Saif. 'We're free, but we're still locked in.'

'No, we're not,' said Yasmin. She had been standing at the door, with a page from her sketch-book pushed through the crack underneath it, and had used a hairpin to jiggle inside the lock. The key on the other side had fallen with a thud and she had used the paper to drag it inside, holding it up with a dramatic flourish.

'That's all very well,' Saif chided. 'But Mr Jhoot is a billionaire – he has money, bodyguards, weapons – and the Egg, which he's probably locked away in the fortress's dungeons! We're six kids from the railways and slums, and Kai's Grandmother is with us of course.' He bowed elegantly.

Kai's Grandmother laughed.

Saif blushed. 'So what can we do?'

Ajay looked around. Saif was right. Mr Jhoot had everything – wealth, power, ruthlessness . . .

What resources do we have?

He took out his mother's pen from behind his ear.

Friends; The Mumbai Sun*; and the Truth.*

Ajay turned the pen slowly in his hand, and stilled.

When he thought about it, not bad odds at all.

He looked at the others, no longer trapped,

energy coursing through his veins and battle-light in his eyes.

'He's got a plan,' said Saif comfortably.

'Here we go,' whistled Jai.

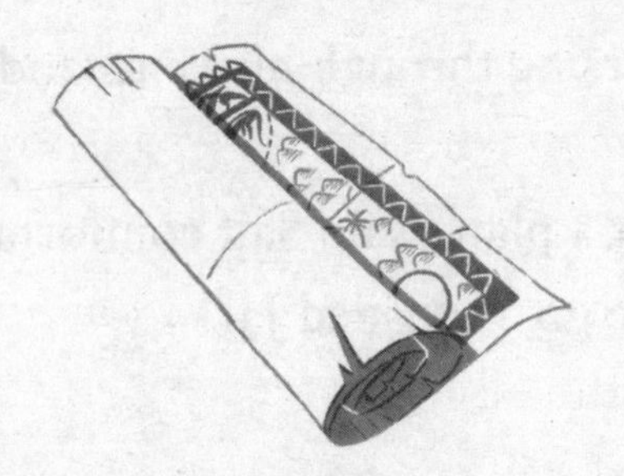

49

Ajay and Saif ran up the steps two at a time to the roof of the fort. The others had stayed behind. Kai's Grandmother still struggled to move easily, and the guards would call through the door in shifts that went every two hours.

'We'll make enough noise for the guards to think we're all here,' Kai's Grandmother had said. *'And disarm them. Then we'll find you.'*

It would also give Yasmin time to chisel a stone egg.

The torches had been lit, and flamed Ajay and Saif's way up the sandstone staircase. Halfway up they saw an open door. In it was a printing press, with piles upon piles of copies of *The Happy*

Paper next to it. Ajay did a double take. *The Happy Paper*? What were copies of *The Happy Paper* doing here? They were in a desert fort – not a newspaper office! Ajay looked at a copy of the paper, and almost fell over in shock.

'Captured railway gang confesses to stealing Mr Jhoot's Treasure!'

Underneath the headline was a photo of them all in chains, being led to court.

'An AI fake,' said Saif in disgust. 'It's not a real photo – just one that looks as if it is.'

Ajay's tongue stuck to the roof of his mouth. He checked the date – it was for tomorrow, the day of the Auction. But how could the paper know that they had been captured?

And then everything made sense.

Mr Jhoot is behind The Happy Paper.

And just as quickly as the first thought came the second.

No wonder it's been supporting him.

The copy he was holding crackled as Ajay crumpled it into a ball and tossed it into the rubbish where it belonged. Newspapers were about truth and justice! How dare *The Happy*

Paper deal in lies and hate and still pretend it could be called a newspaper?

'We'll come back with the others and deal with *The Happy Paper* once and for all,' he promised. It was a promise to himself as much as Saif. 'Now to the roof – all the other exits will be guarded until Mr Jhoot leaves for the Auction tonight. And tonight will be too late. We need to get a message out to Mumbai now!'

He ran up the remaining stairs with Saif following behind him.

'Why did the roof have to be so high up?' panted Saif.

They pushed open the door. It was evening – usually Ajay's favourite time of day! The time when he could sit on the station steps, helping Vinod grind warm spices for chai, and think about the stories he had written and dream about the ones he would write next. Ajay stood on the roof and breathed in his freedom. The sky was swirled with reds and tints of orange and lemon. Out in front and below them stretched Jaisalmer, the lights in the buildings like sequins scattered on dark velvet.

Saif stopped at a lamp on the roof that could be swung to shine a round spotlight into the air.

He took out the coin Ash had given him, and flicked it up, catching it. 'I have an idea!' he said. 'Go – I'll find you.'

Ajay went to the battlement wall. He looked down and his heart lurched. There were people, going about their lives, happy, unaware of Mr Jhoot and the way he was terrorizing everyone Ajay cared about. The sense of freedom and joy vanished, and Ajay felt sick. He needed help. He had thought he would be able to shout for it – but they were too high up. No one on the ground was going to hear them. Saif tapped him on his shoulder.

'Look up at the signal I made,' said Saif behind him, looking inordinately pleased with himself. 'It's like the bat signal, but better.'

Ajay looked, and gasped. Shining into the sky, through a paper cut-out Saif had put over the light, was a signal: a spot of bright light shaped like the falcon on Ash's coin!

'Do you think Ash will see it?' Saif's face was suddenly wistful as he looked at the signal shining on to the sky already pricked by early starlight.

Ajay swallowed and was about to reply when in the sky he saw a shadow flying around the fort. Not a superhero! Not a plane! A bird, flying towards them as if it had been called by the light of the lamp! Ajay jumped up in glee. Ali the camel rider's falcon! It circled three times, shimmering in the dusky light. Ajay used the three-note whistle Ali had taught him to call it. The falcon heard him, flew down on to the battlement and began preening itself.

Saif almost toppled over. 'What is that?' he stammered.

'A friend,' said Ajay.

He stood for a second, overwhelmed with a wave of relief and joy.

Then he started scribbling a message to Ali to send to Emmanuel and also Mr Gupta – the gruff editor of *The City Paper*, and the only person Ajay knew in Mumbai with enough power and integrity to enter Mr Jhoot's secret rooms. He folded it small enough to fit under the ring around the falcon's leg, keeping his fingers as far as he could from its terrifying beak and talons.

'Thank you, friend,' Ajay said softly.

He let the falcon go so that it flew up and up into the rose-pink clouds, carrying his message – and his hopes – back to Ali to pass on.

The first part of the plan – getting help and gathering the troops – was complete.

Now for the second: The Heist!

50

It was nearly evening. Ajay and Saif were standing, feeling very small, at the entrance to the fortress's dungeons. Ajay was holding a replica of the Egg. Yasmin had chiselled it and proudly given it to him when she and the others had found them, before going to get the printing press ready.

'Ajay, I am an apprentice engineer,' grumbled Saif. 'I am not a thief.'

'We have to get the Egg, brother Saif – we can't risk it being taken out of India! And taking back what is rightfully yours is not theft, or at least,' Ajay amended, 'it shouldn't be.' Before Saif could argue further, Ajay turned back to the entranceway. His skin tingled. It was shadowy and cold, and there were two security cameras pointed at the locked iron gate that beeped and flashed red in a disconcerting way.

Saif looked up and squinted. 'Infrared cameras,' he said.

'How do we get past them?' Ajay asked.

Before Saif could answer, thudding heavy boots echoed down the corridor. Ajay and Saif ducked into the shadows as two of Mr Jhoot's bodyguards marched past the gate with torches, checking it. 'All clear?' said one.

'All clear,' confirmed the other guard in a scrapey voice, then chuckled. 'Don't know why we bother. Not as if anyone's getting past the blazing lasers.' The guard thumbed inside the gate, and they both laughed.

Ajay and Saif looked at each other in consternation. Lasers?

The guards walked past them, one saying to the other: 'Ten minutes to break. The next lot better not be late for their shift.'

Ajay squeezed Saif's shoulder. 'Ten minutes to get past the cameras, the lock and the lasers. You can do it, Saif!'

Saif turned to give him a look, which thankfully Ajay couldn't see in the darkness.

A couple of minutes later, Saif and Ajay marched towards the gate, one behind the other, under a heavy woollen rug from the corridor that was draped over them both.

'Are you sure this will work?' said Ajay, holding on to Saif's shoulders, as he blindly walked forwards.

'Of course it will work!' Saif snapped in front of him. 'Our body heat is being trapped by the rug. No thermal imaging cameras can detect it. Ow! My nose!'

Ajay winced in sympathy – Saif must have bumped into the iron gate!

With a stream of indignant complaints, Saif started work on picking the lock. The sound of clanking and clanging filled the air.

'Are you done yet?' asked Ajay anxiously, after what seemed like hours.

'I am picking an ancient lock, under a blanket, in the dark,' Saif said irritably. 'I am an apprentice engineer, not a miracle worker!'

There was a sudden ping as the catch on the

lock released, a sigh of relief from Saif, and the door swung open. They shuffled out from under the rug, and ducked inside the gate where the cameras were no longer pointing at them.

Ajay shivered. In front of him was a web of hot, red lasers emanating from metal jets. In the distance, through the web, lit up by the neon-red lights, a small glimpse of the dinosaur's Egg, black as night, peeping through.

'It's OK, Saif!' said Ajay, more confidently than he felt, seeing the burning lasers between him and the Egg. It was so tantalizingly close! 'All we have to do is manoeuvre ourselves through the beams!'

With a frown of distrust, Saif flicked one of his playing cards into the room. It got caught by the lasers. There was a smell of a burnt chapati, as the card scorched, sizzled and charred. With a puff, it disintegrated into a flare of red and gold sparks and fell into smoky grey ash.

Saif watched it and gulped. 'This is not a good plan for me. You go ahead – I'll wait and stand guard.'

There was no other choice! Holding the package Yasmin had given him firmly, like a mighty

Japanese rugby player holding a rugby ball, Ajay edged forwards. The first hot laser was a horizontal line at chest level. Ajay took a deep breath and, sweating, crawled under it. His eyes watered from the heat. The next beams crisscrossed. Ajay twisted through, then did a dive over the next one.

'Ajay – slow down!' yelped Saif.

Ajay, feeling a sudden flare of heat and lacerating pain on his arm, looked down. The edge of the laser had caught his shirt. A flame was tearing through the corner of it so that the edges burnt black and crinkled. Ajay blew on the singed spot and breathed a sigh of relief when the flame blew out. A little charcoal smoke twisted upwards.

His brow damp with sweat, Ajay looked ahead again. He could see the Egg through the final two beams. One beam was at neck height; the other was at ankle height. He slowly made his way through. There was the rancid smell of burnt hair on top of his head, there and gone again.

And then – finally – he was in front of the Egg.

It was bigger than he remembered. Even more magnificent! Once again, his love of dinosaurs stirred through him. A memory shone: of finding some plastic model dinosaurs in a bin at the station and playing with them on the station steps – even though two were broken and had no heads. They were as exciting as dragons, and real!

Ajay took out Yasmin's sculpture.

'Quickly, Ajay!' Saif's voice was filled with terror. 'There's no time!'

'One . . . two . . . three!' Ajay whispered to himself. In one quick movement, he slipped the Egg into his right hand, as he replaced it with Yasmin's sculpture with his left.

For a second, breathless, he waited.

Silence!

The alarm hadn't been activated. The Egg was his. Ajay stared at it in his hands. The Egg lay heavy. The rough surface of it grazed his skin, and for a moment he thought of it not as a fossil, but as a container – something that held life. What if millions of years ago it had cracked open, releasing a baby dinosaur?

'Ajay!' screamed Saif, his voice shredded with panic.

The guards!

Ajay was jolted back to the present. He had to

get back – do everything in reverse – and this time holding the Egg. He took a deep breath. He was editor of *The Mumbai Sun*. He could do this.

He hurried back, twisting and bending through the lasers, precariously balancing the Egg in his right hand. Through the lasers he could see Saif jumping up and down in agitation. It was almost time for the next shift. Ajay held his breath until he got to the last laser. He was almost through. He knelt to go under it when the concrete floor echoed with the stomping of boots outside.

'The guards!' Saif hissed before bolting out of sight behind a pillar.

Ajay froze underneath the laser.

The guards were coming closer. Their shadows were almost at the gate. He could see the lights from the torch beams falling this way and that.

'Look sharp!' he heard one say.

There was a sound from behind the pillar.

'What's that?'

Ajay saw the guards' backs as they turned sharply, their torches shining on it. Ajay got ready to run out to save Saif.

Another sound. A grey rat scurried out from

behind the pillar.

The guards stopped. Laughed. Lowered their torches.

'Nothing to worry about except vermin. Come on – let's get out of here,' said the first guard.

As the guards continued on their shift, Ajay ran out to join Saif who was crouched and trembling with relief. They hid in the shadows, panting at their narrow escape.

'That was close,' said Ajay, wiping the sweat from his forehead.

'What now, Ajay?' whispered Saif next to him from the shadows. He had taken the Egg from Ajay and was clutching it in awe.

Ajay felt his heart race. It was time. He took his mother's pen from behind his ear and held it out in front of him. Its gold nib seemed to shine, even in the darkness. In its own way, at least to him, the pen was as precious as the dinosaur's Egg. Ajay tightened his hand around its barrel. Resolve straightened his spine.

'It's the night before the Auction,' Ajay said softly. 'As soon as Mr Jhoot and his guards leave to prepare for it, we slip out to the market and put out a call to the railway kids here. I have a mission for them.'

'And while we wait?' Saif asked.

'What else?' Ajay gripped his mother's pen and felt confidence course through his veins. He smiled grimly.

'We prepare for battle.'

It was time to write – and print – the very latest edition of *The Mumbai Sun*.

51

It was the day the whole of India had been waiting for. The day the Auction was to be held outside in the desert.

Helicopters from around the world had been flying into Jaisalmer since morning, billowing up clouds of rust-red sand in the process. Crooks', the International Auction House, had built a huge stage, and on it were the auctioneer and Trustees from The Big Museum in England, mingling and laughing together.

The guests were delighted by the desert camp – huge, decorated tents, richly embroidered scarlet rugs, torchlight, jazz music and a hooded street magician with a small assistant, who wandered in between the tables entertaining them. Every one of the guests had been given a folded copy of *The Happy Paper* on arriving.

Mr Jhoot, laughing and smiling and taking photos with the guests, bounded up on the stage.

There was a thunderous round of applause.

'Welcome! Welcome! You are here today for the event of a lifetime!' said Mr Jhoot. 'As many of you will know, a little while ago I was attacked by a gang known as *The Mumbai Sun*.'

'I read about them – utterly terrifying,' said one guest, in a low voice to another.

'This gang stole a treasure map from me,' Mr Jhoot continued, his brow deeply furrowed. 'Happily they've been caught, and, using the treasure map,' he took a deep breath, 'I have discovered the Treasure of Thar.'

There was a burst of applause from the audience – a palpable sense of excitement all around. It was as if the air itself had become thick with gold.

'Now, many of you will be wondering, why did I spend my life seeking the Treasure of Thar? When I was young, my father gave me the treasure map and told me that one day I would be the one to find it.' Mr Jhoot's voice went teary with remembrance. 'After decades of searching, that day has finally come. A dinosaur Egg, worth billions of rupees! And now on sale to the highest bidder.'

'I'll buy it,' said an American politician.

'No, me!' said a Trustee from The Big Museum.

'Surely we should see it first?' said someone in the crowd.

Mr Jhoot nodded. 'Of course.' He gestured to one of the bodyguards and rubbed his hands with glee. 'Let me do the honours.' He took hold of the velvet cloth over the glass case and pulled it off with a swish. There was thunderous applause.

'Excuse me,' said the tiny assistant, who had been shadowing the hooded street magician.

Everyone watched as the assistant clambered on to a chair.

'That egg's a fake.'

A ripple of shock went through the guests.

The magician's assistant uncovered his head. The cloak fluttered in a gust of wind, as his small face took on an expression of serene, all-knowing wisdom. Unable to help himself, he looked directly at Mr Jhoot and added with supreme satisfaction, 'Just like you!'

It was Kai.

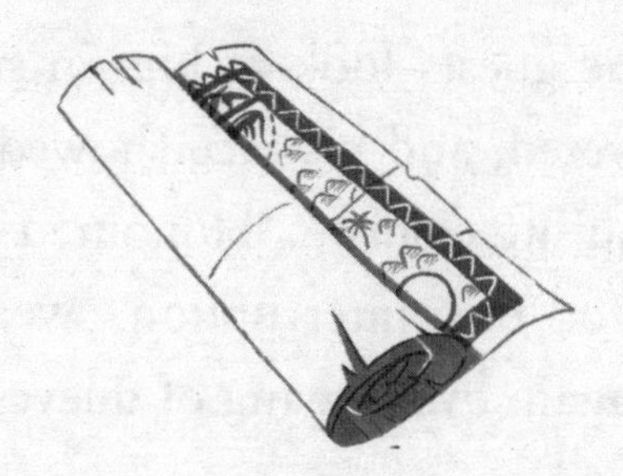

52

'How dare you?' said Mr Jhoot.

'Check, why don't you?' said Kai, gleefully. 'See for yourself.'

The auctioneers carefully took the egg out. One looked at Mr Jhoot in consternation. 'He's right. It's a fake all right – made of stone. An excellent replica.'

'Of course it is excellent,' said Yasmin, stepping forward from the crowd, uncovering her hood, so that her hair fell down in waves, her green eyes glinting as she gave a bow. 'I made the sculpture myself.'

Mr Jhoot looked like he was going to have a fit. 'You were meant to be locked up.'

Seeing the guests look at him in surprise, Mr Jhoot recovered, and his face showed an expression of exquisite distaste. 'Honoured guests. I do apologize for this interruption. We have been infiltrated again by the gang of thieves called *The Mumbai Sun*.'

There was an explosion on the stage.

And suddenly the crowd's attention was caught. From the explosion burst a cloud of purple smoke with sparkling stars of light – and Ajay!

Saif, in his hooded magician's robe, stepped back, clapping the clouds of dyed flour from his hands, looking inordinately proud of himself.

'I am Ajay, editor of *The Mumbai Sun*!' said Ajay (with his new haircut, courtesy of the laser beams), coming to the centre of the stage. He turned to the crowd and took a deep breath. 'And I'm here to tell you we aren't thieves. We're railway kids who run a newspaper. Shake your copies of *The Happy Paper*.' He shook a copy to demonstrate.

There was a flapping all around them, and one by one each guest found a pink copy of *The Mumbai Sun* (courtesy of the printer in the fort) slipping into their hand. There was a murmur of pleasure. As there should be – the copies of *The Mumbai Sun* that they held were the best editions ever! Yasmin had outdone herself with the illustrations of dinosaurs that moved through the pages like a flick-book!

Ajay turned to the crowd and said softly: 'Listen as we tell you the true story of the Treasure of Thar,' and called Kai's Grandmother to the stage. Vinod and Jai helped her on and stood to one side. She stood in front of Mr Jhoot and the

Trustees, and she told them the story of the Guardians and their quest to keep the Treasure safe from the British.

One of the Trustees of The Big Museum in England cut in pompously. 'The British did not *steal* during colonial times. Items were freely given . . .'

'Nothing "given" during colonial times was done freely,' said a familiar voice from the musicians' stand. Ajay looked joyfully around. 'If I give you something when you have a gun to my head, is that freely given? Or is it extortion?' Emmanuel had stepped forward from where he had been playing the wonderful jazz music.

Ajay waved at him. 'Emmanuel! Ali passed you my message?'

'Wouldn't have missed this for the world,' smiled Emmanuel.

'But we keep things safe,' whined the Trustee. 'You are still a developing country. You cannot—'

'First, you refuse to return items that are stolen and rightfully belong to India, then you patronize us by suggesting that we can't keep our own heritage safe?' Kai's Grandmother's voice was low and dangerous. 'That is perilously similar to the belief that colonizing was a "civilizing" influence. We are not children—'

Vinod coughed. She looked at him. 'Some of us are,' whispered Vinod to her.

Kai's Grandmother smiled, then turned back. 'Or rather, we are not fools,' she ended.

Ajay nodded. Then continued. 'The Guardians kept the Treasure safe from being looted by the British. The first *The Mumbai Sun* heard about the Treasure of Thar was when Kai came to us with his map.'

'A pack of lies,' cut in Mr Jhoot. He turned to them. 'You have read *The Happy Paper*. You know that the map belongs to me,' he said again.

'You *own The Happy Paper*,' Ajay laughed. 'Of course it's going to support you.'

Mr Jhoot shook his head. 'You really need to be more pragmatic, Ajay,' he hissed. 'Deal with the world as it is, rather than as you wish it would be. Watch and learn.'

And a heartbeat too late, Ajay realized that Mr Jhoot might win after all.

53

Mr Jhoot turned to the guests. 'You have heard from the railway gang. Now hear from me – because that is what we are, aren't we? A rational, modern society that is able to debate?'

There was a murmuring of agreement.

Mr Jhoot smiled. 'So, let me begin. Railway gangs loot and pillage across India. They threaten our very way of life, take our jobs, harm our children, lie for profit, scrounge . . .'

Each word hammered at Ajay. He wanted to shut his ears, to stop the attack. It felt like it had when he had been drowning under the sand. He watched the crowd slowly harden against him and his friends, and his heart was filled with dread.

'I invited a railway gang into my home, and what did they do? Steal. Rob . . .'

The crowd was getting more hostile now, and Ajay was reminded of the stones thrown at Jai and Kai on the lake.

Mr Jhoot looked as if he were soaking the hostility in – as if he was energized by it. He kept his eyes on the crowd, but in a voice, like a hiss or a gentle rattle, that only Ajay could hear, said softly, 'Don't you see, Ajay? I was always going to win. The truth makes people uncomfortable; lies are what people *want* to believe.'

Ajay shuddered.

Then he lifted his head.

Mr Jhoot was wrong!

Ajay stood in front of the crowd. 'How can you believe all these lies? How can you not stand up for us? Mr Jhoot is the head of a crime organization: the four-headed snake—'

'Nonsense,' smiled Mr Jhoot. 'You're imagining things, Ajay.'

'Hardly,' said a gruff voice from the crowd.

Mr Jhoot looked startled.

Mr Gupta, the legendary editor of *The City*

Paper, and Ajay's friend, stepped forward in a crumpled grey suit.

'You got my message!' Ajay waved to him, relieved.

'Apologies it took me so long to get here,' smiled Mr Gupta in return. Mr Gupta turned to Mr Jhoot and his expression turned stern. 'Mr Jhoot, following Ajay's note, the police found stolen treasures – including a priceless Fabergé egg – hidden in your office in Mumbai.'

Mr Jhoot turned pale.

'The police raid, accompanied by journalists from *The City Paper*, also found papers in your office showing that you are the head of the crime syndicate known as the four-headed snake.'

'That's not possible,' the auctioneer, from the international auction house, Crooks', started to mumble. 'Mr Jhoot is a revered man in the world of art. Some mistake, surely?'

'None at all,' said Mr Gupta coolly, directing a level glance at the auctioneer. 'Actually, your organization's directors are also wanted by the police. The legal raid of Mr Jhoot's office found evidence that Crooks' has deliberately turned a blind eye to selling stolen treasures.'

'Papers! Documents!' said Mr Jhoot. 'What other evidence do you have?'

'Plenty,' said Ajay, smiling broadly. 'I did a lot of interviews last night!'

And out of the crowd stepped people from the slums who, one by one, spoke about how Mr Jhoot and the four-headed snake had coerced them into giving up their most precious heirlooms. Ajay had put out a call amongst the railway kids of Jodhpur, Jaipur and Jaisalmer, and they, incensed by the lies of *The Happy Paper*, had responded by investigating every lead they had heard of. They had found out the truth of Mr Jhoot's leech-like behaviour.

As each victim spoke, Mr Jhoot's face tightened. There was no guilt, Ajay realized, suddenly afraid. There was just anger at being caught.

In his mind's eye, Ajay saw the image of a coiled snake ready to strike.

'Don't just stand there!' Mr Jhoot cried to his bodyguards. 'Grab them!'

Bodyguards on the right of the stage stepped forward, carrying weapons – and were stopped by the falcon! It dipped and dived, clawing at their faces, with Ali whistling behind with a wave for Ajay.

Bodyguards on the left of the stage stepped forward – and were stopped by a host of camel riders circling from the sides.

'Nibbles!' Saif cried joyously, as Nibbles kicked one of the bodyguards, about to attack Kai, to the ground. 'The camels must have found their way back to the camp!' Nibbles looked up at Saif, snorting affectionately.

The crowd, furious, took the truncheons off the guards.

Mr Jhoot looked at Ajay.

'You've lost, Mr Jhoot,' said Ajay, as Kai came running up on stage. 'Give up.'

'Didn't you hear me?' Mr Jhoot said softly. 'I never lose.'

He grabbed Kai.

54

'Ajay!' Kai choked.

'Let him go,' said Ajay, running up to Mr Jhoot.

'Oh, I will,' said Mr Jhoot. 'After I escape.' He looked about to move down the steps when an idea seemed to strike him. He turned, like a whip, back to Ajay. 'You had a fountain pen when we last met. I've learnt it is an item of infinite value. Give it to me: a small goodwill gesture to ensure Kai's safety.'

Ajay took out his mother's pen. The only item he owned that belonged to her; the only thing that made her real. For a moment he could see her shadowed eyes as she smoothed down his hair for the last time. His heart hurt.

He hurriedly gave it to Mr Jhoot.

Mr Jhoot held it in his hand, admiring it.

'Let Kai go,' Ajay whispered.

Mr Jhoot was too entranced by the pen. His mistake! There was a blur of feathered wings, as Ali's falcon, having dealt with the bodyguards, came sweeping in and clawed at his arm, drawing blood. Mr Jhoot yelled, and let go of his grip on Kai. Kai was caught and pulled out of the way by Ajay.

'I'll get you!' yelled Mr Jhoot.

'No, you won't,' said a small figure coming up on stage with pink hair.

'Ash!' said Saif in delight. 'You got the falcon-signal!'

Mr Jhoot jammed Ajay's mother's pen into his pocket and turned to her, his face lined, his fists clenched. Ash turned and flung magical cards at him which sparked and flared flames, disorientating him.

Ash grinned at Saif. 'I told you I would find you if you called!'

Mr Jhoot kept moving blindly forwards in a

rage. Saif stepped into place, deftly pickpocketing Ajay's mother's pen from Mr Jhoot's pocket and making it vanish into his own. Mr Jhoot, livid with anger, picked up a truncheon and faced Ajay.

'I'll get you, if it's the last thing I do!' he shouted.

He moved and Kai lunged at his ankles, whilst Ajay lunged at his knees, like a rugby player.

For a moment it looked like even with the two of them it wouldn't be enough – then, with a thundering crash, Mr Jhoot toppled and fell.

Ajay and Kai got up and, like victorious boxers in a ring, high-fived!

Yasmin and Jai came up on the stage holding up the Egg for everyone to see, followed by Vinod, waving pink copies of *The Mumbai Sun*. Then came Ash and Saif, letting forth from their hands dazzling, sparkling clouds of dust. As Ali's falcon circled over them, Ajay and Kai gave a signal. At the signal, they all turned to the crowd, stepped around the fallen figure of Mr Jhoot, and – to the sound of a triumphant string of jazz notes from Emmanuel – bowed!

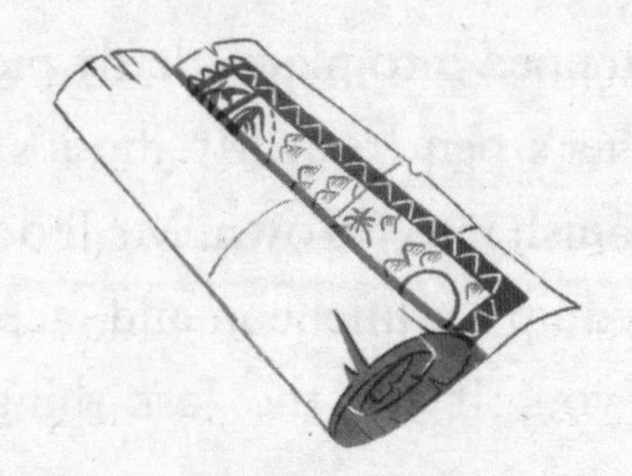

55

Ajay grinned at the others. 'This is the best party ever!'

It was a month later. The sun was still blazing hot and bright, although there were patches of gathering clouds. They had all been invited to the party in the gardens of The National Museum of India, celebrating the new dinosaur Egg exhibit. The gardens were thrumming with the sound of jazz and sitars.

Vinod had done the cooking – mounds of pilau rice with fiery chilli tops to look like volcanoes, dinosaur-shaped rotis, Indian sweets shaped into crystallized dinosaur eggs, even dry ice to create volcanic landscapes!

The Treasure of Thar was in the centre of the garden, secured in a large glass case, for everyone to see for free. Lots of railway kids and slum kids had surrounded it, their eyes wide as they pointed and gasped, and Yasmin gave them charcoal and sheets of paper, teaching them with sure, deft strokes.

Saif and Ash were walking around in silk magician robes doing coin and card tricks.

Kai's Grandmother came over to Ajay, who was looking proudly over the latest copy of *The Mumbai Sun – the Dinosaur Edition*!

'You are pleased?' she said.

Ajay nodded, feeling at one with the world. 'Because of our story, a group of politicians are going to try to pass laws that will make it harder for dinosaur fossils and precious treasures to be stolen from India.'

Kai's Grandmother smiled. 'Dinosaur bones and fossils are precious. They hold within them clues to the changes in Earth itself. Perhaps they will even be able to guide us on how to find a new way to fight climate change.' She looked pensive, and her thoughtful expression rested on where

Kai and Jai were playing catch in the blazing sunlight. 'Ajay, I have another favour to ask.'

He turned to her, surprised.

Her voice trembled. 'My dementia is getting worse, and one day I may no longer be able to look after Kai. If that day happens, will you take care of him?' She turned to him and bit her lip. 'Perhaps it is too big a burden to ask.'

Ajay, his heart swelling, was looking at Kai, who was playing with a wide grin on his face, scampering around as Jai threw the ball. He remembered Kai's jabby feet, and then Emmanuel's words.

To help once is to help always.

Ajay shook his head. 'Kai's not a burden. He's my friend. I'm always there for him. I'll always be there for him.'

Kai's Grandmother put her hand on his shoulder for a moment. Then moved away.

Jai and Kai came over, smiling. So did Yasmin and Saif and Vinod and Ash behind them.

Ajay put his arms around them. 'Look how many copies of *The Mumbai Sun* we've sold!'

There was the sound of thunder in the sky.

He looked up in shock.

'It can't be . . .' said Vinod.

Big raindrops started to splash down, watering the earth that had for so long been dry and parched.

'The end of the heatwave! You'll be able to play cricket again!' said Kai to Jai, who tousled his hair, suddenly looking filled with ebullient joy.

As the rain splashed down, and Ajay used *The Mumbai Sun* as shelter for them all, Kai turned from where he had been looking at the Egg and shouted. 'Look up!'

They all looked up as one. A winged shadow was flying over them. Ajay held his breath. In the distance it looked like a dragon – soaring.

ACKNOWLEDGEMENTS

To all my friends – thank you for everything, always, but especially this year. I am the luckiest person in the world to have you in my life.

To Lou Kuenzler and everyone I have known from the workshops – thank you for all the support and help and for the character of Kai! As always, the book could only have been written with you there.

To Zoe, Gav, Oscar, Tilly, Joanne, Jock, Samantha, Alistair, Katie, Stacy, Freddie, Matt, Hayley, the Westons, the Ruffles, Peter and Wendy Watts, Yoko, Chris, Hiroto, Yuki, Euri, Helena, Amit, Satchi, Tushin, Kajal, Neha, Nikhil, Meera, Savan, Mitul, Nishma, Nahid, Eva, Priyesh, Hema, Vijal, Urvina, Cath, Jo, Hannah, Beth, Kate, Paula, Vicky, Deborah, Rob, Clara, Carys, Jaya, Anjali, Aarti and family, Jaimika, Nick, Tosin, Claudia, Francesca, Simran, Alexandra, Alex, Zoe, Andrew, Jocelyn, Jonathan, Jon, Pru 7-10L, 7F, Tanav, Florence and family, Amina, Savannah, Bob, Chris, the basketball players. My friends in Kurayoshi and Amqui.

To Barry Cunningham, Rachel, Rachel, Esther, Elinor, Jazz, Liv, Ruth and Emily and everyone at Chicken House for championing this book and being so incredibly supportive and giving of your expertise – thank you for making dreams come true. To Kathy – you are utterly amazing. To Magness Editorial for proofreading my books so wonderfully.

And finally, to all the students I have taught – wherever you are I wish you kindness, tenderness and joy.

Ajeet Prabu/Sidney Sarpong

Varsha Shah always dreamt of being a writer. After studying Law at Cambridge University, she worked as a solicitor and has written articles for various publications. She is now an English teacher, and has taught English as a foreign language in both Japan and Canada. She loves travelling and is completely obsessed with basketball.

TRY ANOTHER GREAT BOOK FROM CHICKEN HOUSE

DARWIN'S DRAGONS by LINDSAY GALVIN

-1835-

Cabin boy Syms Covington is on the voyage of a lifetime to the Galapagos Islands with the world-famous scientist Charles Darwin. But when Syms falls overboard during a huge storm, he washes up on an unexplored island. Stranded there, he makes a discovery that could change the world . . .

Now it's not just his own survival at stake – the future of an undiscovered species is in his hands.

A striking and original adventure . . .
just the sort of story I love.
EMMA CARROLL

Paperback, ISBN 978-1-912626-46-5, £7.99 • ebook, ISBN 978-1-913322-15-1, £7.99